Prissy DuPonce

~ o ~

A Prisstine Prissy Prissentation

Book One

Prissy DuPonce

~ o ~

A Prisstine Prissy Prissentation

Book One

By

Grant Howie

Published in Australia in 2014/2021 by;
Trenwick House Publishing
www.trenwickhouse.com.au

ISBN 978-0-9803867-2-1

Cover photogrpahy: © 2014, D Clarke Photography
www.dclarkephotogpraphy.com.au

Cover design: © 2014, Trenwick House

Printed by;
Lightning Source

National Library of Australia
Cataloguing-in-Publication entry;
Author: Howie, Grant, author.
Title: Prissy DuPonce : the story of an accidental drag queen / Grant Howie ; D Clarke, photographer.
ISBN: 9780980386721 (paperback)
Subjects: Female impersonators--Fiction.
Other Authors/Contributors:
Clarke, Darren, photographer.
Dewey Number: A823.4

Dedicated to;

Kim W.
Who made me finish this book in less than a year.
... well, almost.

1. Who'd a Thunk?

Alex and I stepped from the pink limo when it had stopped at the curb. The door was opened for us by an exquisitely dressed drag queen, wearing a short white silk skirt, with several layers of tulle underneath. Over the top of the dress, she wore a red ringmaster's jacket, replete with tails and black top hat and gloves. Black fishnet stockings and bright red shoes with four-inch heels finished the look. Mum and Nate followed us out of the limo and we walked along the red carpet.

Alex leaned in close to me. 'I've just spotted Roman up ahead. I don't deal well with the media.'

'Roman?' I queried.

'Roman Tolliday, the presenter, from JAY FM,' responded Alex.

I smiled at him. 'Okay, dear. I'll talk to him. You take Mum and Nate inside.'

'Thanks, sweetie.' Alex kissed me on the cheek and walked rapidly past Roman's position as I approached him.

'Peter Long-Smith, can you share a word for our listeners and readers?' Roman asked.

'Good evening, Roman,' I replied. 'I think we can spare a word or two.'

'That's fantastic, Peter,' responded Roman. 'What's it like to be nominated in so many categories?'

'It's rather incredible really,' I answered, the mic millimetres from my mouth. 'Technically, I haven't been nominated for anything, only Alex has. That said, neither of us feel we've done anything special.'

'That's not what I've heard, or seen,' responded Roman. 'What's with this technical spin? You do know that I know?'

'I do, I think?'

'Isn't that why you're here and not Prissy DuPonce?'

'I'm not sure I do know what you mean, Roman.' I smiled.

'Aren't you Prissy?'

'Am I? I'm not sure where you heard that.'

'From what I've heard, you and Prissy are never at the same venue at the same time, but Alex is usually where Prissy is.'

'At least I know you've been to see the shows?' I asked.

'I was there on opening night for the new venue and I've seen Prissy perform on many other occasions. I must admit she is my favourite.'

'Thank you.'

'Why do you think she's so popular?'

'How long's a piece of string?' I countered. 'I honestly don't know. She's witty, sometimes. She knows how to have fun with her audiences.'

'Don't I know it. Why does she sing live though? Wouldn't it be easier to mime?'

'She sings because she can, although she doesn't always. It depends on the song. Mind you the band doesn't like it when she mimes.'

'I bet they hate it,' laughed Roman.

'I should get inside.' I began to move on from where Roman stood.

'Peter, could you write an article about how it all began?' called Roman as I entered the building.

'I'll think about it, Roman. Don't call me, I'll call you.'

I greeted more people in the entry hall, where I caught up with Alex, Mum and Nate. We pushed through to the main hall to find our tables. We were handed programs and I began to flip though mine. As we approached, I saw some of our closest friends sitting or milling about. The Poncettes and their partners were at a table next to where Alex and I were sitting.

'This is embarrassing,' I said when I realised where our table was. 'Do they know something we don't?

'Why's that, Pete?' inquired Alex.

'Look, we're almost at the front,' I indicated. 'Like they know we're going to collect.'

'Don't be silly. It's just the way they set the tables.'

'I dunno,' he responded doubtfully.

'How dare they be nominated for so many awards,' declared the drag queen with chopsticks sticking out of her tall black wig and waving a Chinese fan in front of her face.

'Who do they think they are?' said an older man with her, brandishing a hand laden with gold rings. Their disdain was palpable.

'I must admit Bitch of the Year would be an appropriate award for her to win,' stated another drag queen, deliberately flicking her large feather boa at me. 'Look what she did to poor Freda at MydSumma this year.'

I so wanted to say something, however was stopped – not by myself, but by an unknown defender at a nearby table.

'Look here, scrag, Prissy was nothing other than professional that day,' responded a man at the table next to ours. I smiled as I sat down.

'Oh puh-lease,' responded the drag queen, looking down her nose at him. 'Prissy humiliated the woman. She's in retirement now because of her. I suppose you were there,' she added laughing into the ear of the thin young man at her side.

'Yes, I was, actually,' stated my unknown defender staunchly.

The drag queen looked a little miffed at having drawn

swords with an eyewitness. She tutted at the man and turned her back on him, swinging her boa deliberately in his face.

Mum leaned in to me. 'They can't say that!' she said indignantly.

'Leave it, Mum, they're point scoring,' I replied. 'They do it all the time. You mean to tell me that you've never engaged in anything like that at the trade shows you attend with your industry colleagues?'

'Well I never,' she responded haughtily.

'Don't give me that, my dear,' I said. 'Who do you think I learnt it from?'

Just then, the lights flickered and faded. 'Here we go gang,' I said nervously. Alex squeezed my hand and the ceremony began.

* * * * *

Alex and I arrived home about eight in the morning, from the after party at the Buckingham Hotel we owned (but more on that later) and staggered through the door. We'd sent Nate home with Mum not long after we arrived at the Buckingham. Alex, having celebrated a little more than me, went straight to bed. The thoughts racing through my brain were going so fast I don't think I would've had any chance of going to sleep. I sat in our rooftop garden, coffee in one hand, sunglasses perched securely on my nose and a plate of very greasy bacon and eggs at my side. Oh, and the headache pills were nearby.

As I lay on the deck chair, the early morning sun warming my skin, I pondered the night before. The thing that had been going over and over in my mind was the one small question from the presenter, Roman, as we entered.

'Peter, could you write us an article about how it all began?'

There's no way an article would do Prissy justice. She needed more than that.

I sat up, took a sip of the coffee, and began eating the

bacon and eggs.

What she needs is ... is ... is ...

* * * * *

Taking a moment to stretch and give my eyes a rest from staring at my laptop, I began to hear the life that had been going on around me all day. In addition, I was back on the sunlounge again, as it was under the shade of the large market umbrella we had in the rooftop garden. It was at that point I heard my name being called.

'Peter, are you up here?' came Alex's slightly exasperated voice.

'Yes, sweetie, I'm up here.'

'What are you doing up there?' said Alex, climbing the stairs to the garden on the roof.

'When you went to bed, I came up here with coffee and breakfast.'

'Have you been here all day?'

'What time is it?'

'Four.'

'Then, yes, I have been here all day.'

'You're mad.'

'Might have to agree with you. I've decided to write a book leading up to last night.'

'I see. When did you decide to do this?'

'Today.'

'What gave you the idea for such a ludicrous project?' Alex sat down and stretched out on the other sun lounge.

'Not what, who,' I replied.

'Okay, I'll play,' said Alex. '*Who* gave you the idea for such a ludicrous project?'

'The radio presenter from last night.'

'Roman? How do you figure that?'

'Well, after you left me to speak to him,' I began.

'You offered!'

I chuckled. 'Well, after you left me, I chatted to him. As I was leaving to come inside, he asked if I'd write an article for him about how it all began.'

'Then what?' Alex leaned on one elbow to face me.

'That's it. Well, when I was sitting here this morning with my greasy breakfast and coffee, I couldn't stop thinking about his question. The more I thought about it, the more I realised that no article could contain Prissy …'

'… so you decided to write a book.'

'Now you're getting it.'

'When do you intend to fit that in?'

'I'll write in my spare time. I'm not working full-time anymore.'

'You're not, huh? So, helping to run the Buckingham, Bucky's (more on that later too) *and* produce Prissy's shows, doesn't keep you busy enough?'

'There is that, and I won't neglect you my love. I'll do it when I feel the inspiration and I know I have a spare hour or two.'

'We'll see.'

'It should be easy from here though; I've spent the day jotting down an outline of what happened. I'll go back and fill it all in and then see what it looks like.' I pointed to my laptop on the end of my lounge.

Alex grabbed the computer and turned it so he could see the screen. 'You do realise that I shall remind you of your obligations if it starts to take over?'

'I should hope you would.'

Alex sat up and I took back my laptop. 'What do you want for dinner?'

'I don't feel like cooking, still getting over last night.'

'Same here.'

'What about some fish and chips?'

'We haven't had that in ages.'

'Excellent. I'll finish up here and we'll see what's about.'

'Cool.'

'Is Nate awake yet?'

'He'd wanna be. Part of the reason we sent him home early with Evelyn was because he still had school today,' said Alex. 'He should be home soon.'

'Speaking of whom, where is mother dearest?' I queried.

'I haven't seen her downstairs,' replied Alex. 'Perhaps she went out.'

'Shopping,' I said without looking up.

Alex laughed and went back downstairs.

Reading back over my notes, the challenge was clearly before me.

There were occasions when Alex and I wondered if we'd made the right decisions.

2. The Committee

Everything began to change when I was seconded on to the committee to plan the end of year function for my company. My colleagues knew I was gay (not that there was a problem) and they wanted to know if I knew any drag queens that might be interested in providing the entertainment for us.

'Why a drag queen?' I asked.

'My husband talked about his recent staff function the other night and they had one. He said everyone loved it,' said Sally.

'Peter, you're gay, can you find us one?' asked Carmen.

'Why a drag queen?' I repeated.

'Why not?' asked Carmen.

'Sounds like fun,' said Sally.

'It'd be different,' added Nick.

'What if people don't like it? Have you seen a drag queen in action yourself?'

'No.'

'I haven't seen one, personally.'

'Right! If you're serious about this, we'll go and see a show tomorrow night. All of us. Bring your partners. I know a place we can go to.'

For some reason, there was hesitation all of a sudden.

'I really believe we should see a show first, to make sure.'

I wasn't totally surprised at the uncomfortable silence.

'I'll meet you outside RP's in Richton at nine-thirty. The first show is at ten-thirty. We can have a few drinks first. You can leave after the show and we can talk again Monday.'

There was half-hearted agreement from the rest of the committee.

'If you're not serious, I won't agree to help.'

'But, Peter.'

'No 'but, Peter's'. It sounds like you're turning the need to have a drag queen at our Christmas function into a feather in our corporate cap,' said Peter.

'How can you say that?' said Sally indignantly.

'You won't go and see a show for yourself.' I sat back in my chair, fuming inside.

Thankfully, the meeting was adjourned. At least I had laid the challenge at their feet. I went back to my desk, grabbing a coffee on the way. I must've been muttering under my breath louder than I thought when Nick spoke to me, 'Are you okay?'

'What? Yes. No.'

'Well, which is it? Yes or no?'

'I'd like to know who put me on this blasted committee!'

'Don't look at me.'

I grunted audibly at the frustration I was feeling.

'We just thought it'd be a nice idea,' began Nick.

'Save it Nick.' I raised my hand.

'Damn! I'm gonna lose tonight now,' he said, slumping into a chair.

'Why? What?'

'At squash. We're playing after work.'

'That's right. Good, I can de-frustrate.'

'I'd rather you didn't. I haven't won a game in weeks.'

We drank our coffee in silence for a few minutes.

'Why are you so cut up about it?' ventured Nick.

'Perhaps I am over-reacting.'

'Ya think?'

'It just seems hypocritical. You want a drag queen for the function but don't want to go out and see one in action. If you lot turn up tomorrow night, I'll agree to secure the services of a drag queen, if not, we'll have to think of something else.'

'Fair enough.'

Nick lost at squash that night. I probably should've taken pity on him.

* * * * *

There are times when it's easy to love my Alex. When I got home, he could sense there was something up. I went to the bathroom and had a shower. I came downstairs and began hurling clothes into the laundry with a little more force than I normally would.

'Okay you.' Alex took me by the hand and sat me on the couch. 'Sit here while I get you something to drink.'

'I don't feel like a glass of anything,' I called.

'You're not getting one of those.'

Alex returned a few minutes later with a large mug of steaming hot chocolate, complete with baby marshmallows. I had to smile.

'That's the smile I was looking for,' said Alex.

I leant over and gave him a kiss.

'You need it. Now tell Uncle Alex all about it.'

I told him about the committee meeting and how angry I became, then how I inflicted a crushing defeat upon poor Nick.

* * * * *

We got to RP's at eight-thirty for happy hour and secured a table right at the front. I was going to enjoy my time, even if those from work didn't show up.

Every Saturday night Peachy Keen performed, along with

her regulars and occasional guests. On the wall behind the stage was a large ornate mirror. The ceiling was draped in the six colours of the rainbow that make up the pride flag. Tracer lights ran around the stage and lit up the mirror.

At nine-thirty, I went outside. To say I was surprised was an understatement. Sally, Carmen and Nick had all turned up with their partners.

'You didn't think we'd show, did you?' said Sally.

'Honestly, no, I didn't.'

'After I had coffee with you, I went and spoke to Carmen and Sally about what you said,' explained Nick.

'Oh?'

'We're sorry for giving you the impression that our motives might've been anything other than genuine,' said Sally.

'It's okay, I overreacted,' I replied. 'I'm glad you're here.'

I took them to our table. My colleagues knew Alex and we were soon introduced to their partners. I bought the first round of drinks and we were happily chatting and laughing. The first show began and after the first song, Peachy Keen spotted my colleagues with me.

'I do like the blonde one, Peter my dear,' cooed Peachy eyeing off Barry, Sally's new boyfriend. 'He's such a honey.'

I turned to see Sally grip his arm a little tighter. Barry laughed at the attention.

'I'm a single woman,' added Peachy. 'I've got plenty of room at my place for you sweetie.'

'I'll be fine thanks,' called Barry in return, wrapping an arm around Sally.

'Not even a thought?'

Barry shook his head and smiled.

'Not even a small amount?' queried Peachy, holding her fingers a short distance apart.

'Nor a large one,' replied Barry, holding his hands a good distance apart.

'Ohh!' gasped Peachy. 'Is he really?' she added, looking at

Sally.

Poor Sally, she went bright red, hid in Barry's chest and began hitting me at the same time.

'You bloody lucky girl,' cooed Peachy. 'If you ever get tired of him, give me a call honey.' Peachy waved in our direction. 'He's sooo tall and handsome too,' added Peachy to the rest of the crowd.

Sally had said to me that Barry played local club football and looking at his height and build, I daresay he was in the top five percent. He was obviously not afraid to brag. You can't really hide when you're showering after a game.

After the show, Peachy came to our table. I introduced my friends to her.

'It's nice to meet you all,' said Peachy. 'I hope you realise I was only having a lend of you just now?'

'Didn't bother me,' replied Barry. 'I think I'm big enough to handle it.'

'I have no doubt about that, sweetheart.' Peachy gave Barry a kiss on the cheek.

I was surprised that he didn't flinch.

'Well my sweets, I must go and schmooze some more. You staying for the second show?' queried Peachy. My colleagues responded enthusiastically. 'I love a happy crowd.'

Peachy moved off.

I leaned into Barry. 'I must admit I'm surprised that you've kept your cool so well.'

'Thanks, Peter,' he replied. 'To let you in on a secret, I have a younger brother who's gay and does drag.'

'Really?'

'He lives overseas now, but when we shared a flat in our early twentys, I got used to his friends visiting.'

'Wow, I'm even more surprised now.' I laughed.

'Don't worry, I put a few of them in their place one night. They never tried to hit on me again.'

'Funny about that.'

'Don't get me wrong, I have nothing against gays or those who do drag, I know who I am and I ain't about to change. When Sally said we were coming here tonight, I had no problems at all.'

'I'm glad you came. Cheers.' Barry and I clinked glasses and raced to down the beers we had. I think he was surprised when I beat him.

* * * * *

'Do you want me to say it and get it over with or not?' Alex said as we walked in the door.

'What are you going on about?'

'Do you want me to say it or not?'

'Say what? I have no idea what you're babbling on about.'

'You give me no option then, I have to say it.'

I looked at Alex, wondering what on earth he was saying, 'Say what?'

'I told you so.'

'Bitch.'

'Well, that's rich.'

'I don't need to be reminded.'

'Told you so. Told you so. Told you so.'

'I get the picture. You told me so. Let's just go to bed and drop the subject.'

'Aw, poor Petey has his nose out of joint.'

'I do not!'

Alex laughed.

'I'm going to bed.'

* * * * *

The follow-up committee meeting on Monday was nothing like the previous one.

'Peter, you're finally here,' greeted Sally, a little impatiently

'You did say ten, didn't you?'

'Yes, I did.'

'Then I'm on time.'

'It's okay, Peter, we all got here early and have been talking about last Saturday night.'

'Gotcha. I gather you had a good time?'

'I always have a good time when someone else buys me drinks,' added Nick.

'Peachy has a habit of doing that sometimes,' I replied. 'Especially if friends of friends of hers watch the show.'

'Like us,' said Carmen.

'Like you.'

'Will you help us now, Peter?' asked Sally.

'Yes, I will,' I said enthusiastically.

'This is going to be so much fun.'

'It'll make the official stuff easier to plan.'

'How long before you know who we can get?'

'Do you think we can get Peachy Keen to do it?'

'It's only June. Until we know a date for the function, it'll be hard to secure anyone. I'll make preliminary enquiries.'

'As discussed, we have our tasks. Next month we'll see how we're going,' said Sally.

3. An Outrageous Thought.

'I have no idea where to begin,' I blurted to Alex that night at dinner.

'What are you going on about now?'

'I've been given the task of finding either a drag queen or drag act, or whatever, for the staff function in December.'

'That shouldn't be too difficult. Why don't you ask Peachy?'

'I've already thought of her and some others. I'll have to dig around and get some contact details.'

'The Shoobags have their own website,' said Alex. 'You can also try the websites for the gay mags. They may have contacts.'

'Or we could just trawl the pubs and chat to the acts when they've finished?'

Alex held up his hand. 'You can have that on your own.'

'Gee thanks partner. Nice of you to be so loving and caring.'

'Anytime my sweet.'

When I finished stacking the dishwasher, I searched the net. I was surprised that after only half an hour, I had found details for four more acts. Along with Peachy Keen and The Shoobags, I had contacts for Freda Mingle, Anita Poke, the Randy Mandys and Lucy Lastic. At least I wouldn't have to trawl the pubs.

The following Saturday night, I approached Peachy Keen after her second show. Drink firmly in hand, I asked my question. 'Peachy, do you do corporate functions?'

'Peter, my love, I'd do anything for you,' she replied, leaving a nice big red kiss on my cheek, so Alex told me later.

'I don't have a date yet though.'

'As soon as you can give me a definite date, I can pencil it in.'

By the end of the following week, I'd heard from the other five acts. The Shoobags were interested, as corporate was one of their strengths. Freda Mingle said she wanted to know the date before making any kind of commitment. Lucy, Anita and the Mandys said they didn't do corporate functions.

So, it was all coming down to the date. What would I do if the date was unacceptable?

* * * * *

I sat bolt upright in bed, the Sunday morning after hearing back from the drag acts.

'What's the matter? Are you alright?' asked Alex.

'I'm fine. I've just had the most outrageous thought.'

'What is it?'

'Promise you won't laugh?'

'I hate it when you get like this,' said Alex, rubbing his brow. 'I'll try.'

'What if I created my own drag queen?'

Alex laughed.

'Thanks for that,' I said indignantly and got out of bed.

* * * * *

On Monday morning, I informed Sally at the first available chance. 'So far, I have three prospects, except they all want to know the date.'

'I can help you there. It'll be the second Tuesday in December.'

'Now that I have specific details, I can go back to the acts and see what they can do.'

'Excellent,' said Sally. 'Next month we can start planning some of the specifics.'

That night, I sent the date to the three positive responses. Freda Mingle, whom I hadn't seen perform in quite a few years, responded immediately, saying that the date conflicted with another commitment. Great, I was one down already! Peachy or The Shoobags still hadn't replied, I was hoping one of those two would be available, at least. Alas, it was not to be. The next to cancel was The Shoobags as the date also clashed with another booking. It was not going well.

June raced by with little progress. The night before the next committee meeting, in early July, I received an email from Peachy. I opened the mail and read it quickly. With an opening line of; 'After checking my diary .....', I knew what was coming next. Peachy had to decline as one of her regulars had confirmed they wanted her services for that day. I switched off the computer and stomped down the stairs.

'What's the matter, sweetie?' said Alex glancing up from the TV.

'I have no act for the function. Peachy's declined as well.'

'That's not good.'

'Ya think? What am I going to tell the committee tomorrow?'

'Tell them you're still investigating. If they want more information, explain how drag time works.'

I had to laugh. Drag time is one of the least understood of all the time-frames available. To understand time in relation to the gay community, here is an estimated comparison. There is Standard Time, which the general populace abides by. Then there is Eastern Standard Gay Time (ESGT), which is usually about twenty minutes behind standard time. Next, you have Eastern Standard Drag Time, which can be thirty minutes behind ESGT. Then there's Dan Time. As much as I love Dan, he has a propensity to be late. If you want him at a function by eight, you need to tell him seven so that he arrives by eight; you get the idea.

'I know you're disappointed sweetie, I'm certain an opportunity will present itself that you had not thought of before.'

I snuggled into Alex on the couch. 'I hope so.' I lay there, resting comfortably but not really watching what was on TV.

'What are you thinking about?' said Alex.

'What do you mean?'

'You've been drumming your fingers on my leg for the last ten minutes.'

'Was I? Sorry.'

'It's okay.'

I leant over and kissed him.

'So, what were you thinking?' he repeated.

'I was thinking about drag queens.'

'Anyone in particular?'

'Not really. Well at least not one that exists yet.'

Alex looked at me oddly.

'I was thinking again about creating my own drag queen.'

'Yes, you told me about that idea some weeks ago.'

'And you laughed at me.'

'Why don't we go away for a long weekend?' suggested Alex.

'Why? When?'

'As to why – so you can think about your outrageous idea. As to when, how about the weekend after next?

* * * * *

'So, where are we going?' I asked as we hopped into the car and began our journey.

'It's a surprise,' replied Alex.

'Why? It's not like it's an anniversary or anything.'

'I know.'

'So, where are we going?'

'All in good time,' he said, lovingly patting me on the knee.

'You can be a little frustrating sometimes.'

'Thank you, my sweet little trollop.'

'Okay, if you're going to be like this, what's to drink?'

'I have supplies of wine for when we arrive.'

'Oooh.' I cooed. 'Ah, but wait. How am I supposed to work trashed?'

'Who said you were going to be drinking that much anyway?'

'So it's going to be measured drinking? That's no fun.' I crossed my arms and stared out of the window. 'Are we there yet?'

Alex laughed. 'We've only just left the house.'

'Yeah, and?'

'How about some food?'

'Ooh, ooh, ooh, can I choose where we go?' I said, like I was five or something. Alex shook his head.

'Okay, you can choose.'

'Goody. I choose ... um, which way are we heading?'

'I guess I can tell you that much. We're heading west along the coast.'

'Oooh, a seaside bungalow with an open fire and plenty of places to have fun.'

'We're going there so you can work.'

'You really are turning this weekend away into some sort of restricted enjoyment thingy weekend?'

'Not at all. There'll be times to relax and enjoy where we are, nevertheless you are being taken away for a specific purpose and you're going to do it.'

'I guess you're right.'

'You know I am.'

At least I was keeping Alex entertained. 'Excuuuuse me then.'

'So, where do you want to eat?'

'What about the roadhouse just out of the city?'

'Yeah, we can do that. I can fill up on fuel as well.'

* * * * *

Alex was brilliant with his selection. The cabin we had, whilst part of a property that had several others scattered about, was secluded enough that we hardly saw anyone else. There was a large verandah facing the sea and got plenty of use as I paced up and down it for hours on end thinking. Although it was winter and cold, my mind was going too fast to notice. Alex kept me fuelled with coffee and hot chocolate. We actually swapped places on Sunday morning, as it sprinkled with rain.

He went for a long walk along the beach after breakfast and I enjoyed the warmth of the open fire to work.

'We're going back to the old ways after lunch,' I stated.

'Oh, why's that?'

'I hardly got any work done this morning.'

'That's not good.'

'It was too warm for me. I got too comfortable and sat and stared at the fire most of the morning.'

'That can be a good thing though. You could mull over all the ideas.'

'That's what you'd think, except my mind ended up everywhere else but.'

'Oh dear,' said Alex. 'Well, I'll suffer for the cause and sit in here by the fire reading or whatever I decide to do and you can walk up and down on the freezing cold porch.'

'Thanks sweetie.'

Alex laughed as I moved all my stuff to the table on the porch. Thankfully, it was wide enough that it stayed dry. As I began to work that afternoon, I saw Alex smile, stoke the fire and settle onto the couch. It was then I realised what I'd said at lunch.'

'You could've stopped me you know,' I called in through

the door.

'I wouldn't want to be held responsible for obstructing the flow of creativity.'

'I'll remind you of your *suffering* one day.'

Alex laughed. 'Go work.'

I closed the door, buttoned my jacket to the neck and looked over my notes. At least it'd stopped raining, so I trotted off down to the beach. From inside the cabin, I was sure Alex thought me nuts. As I walked along the beach, I had some brilliant ideas and so I raced up from the beach, mounted the steps two at a time and furiously tapped away at my laptop.

After dinner on Sunday night, Alex successfully tempted me into the spa with him and a large bottle of wine. 'How's the character coming?'

'I think I have her worked out. Thanks for taking me away this weekend.'

'It worked, didn't it?'

'Yeah. After watching Peachy last Saturday night, I felt I could do it myself.'

'You've always loved theatre.'

'I need to go looking for some clothes. I have some finessing to do before there's a revelation.'

'I'm looking forward to it.'

We arrived home just after lunch on Monday and I called the man who, after applying make-up, becomes Peachy, 'Hi Karl, its Peter Long-Smith.'

'Hi, Pete, what's on your mind?'

'As you know, Peachy can't do my staff function at the end of the year...'

'..Yeah, sorry about that...'

'..Nah, that's okay, it's worked out well. I've decided to create my own drag queen.'

'Good for you.'

'I've just spent the weekend conceiving her. I won't give too much away just yet.'

'I understand. What did you want to know?'

'I was hoping to steal a few trade secrets from you, if that's okay?'

Karl laughed heartily. 'I'm sorry, Pete, that wasn't meant personally. I've never heard it put that way before.'

'What way?'

'That you're asking to steal some trade secrets. Most guys don't ask they just steal.'

We spoke for almost two hours. I put Karl on speaker so I could write more easily. 'Thanks Karl, this is great. When it's time, I'd like to make my debut at RPs.'

'Let me know when you're ready.'

'I will. Bye.'

'How did that go?' asked Alex as I came into the lounge.

'Very well. I wrote down three pages of notes, ideas and tips. It was great. I asked to debut her at RPs and all I have to do is let Karl know when I'm ready.'

'What a night that will be.'

4. The Shape of Things to Come.

I began immediately to teach myself how to apply make-up and to find the right 'look' I wanted. I couldn't settle on one, so I just continued to play around. Another aspect of the character was the chest. Again, I began experimenting. Having worked on proto-types for the enhancement of my chest, I rang a good friend for assistance.

'Hey, Chrissy,' I said when the voice answered.

'Hi, Petey, how's it going?' she replied.

'Busy.'

'Yeah, what else is new?'

We laughed.

'I need a favour.'

'Sure.'

'I need you to check out some breasts for me.'

For a moment, there wasn't a sound.

'Chrissy?'

'I'm here.'

'Are you okay?'

'No.'

'Oh.'

'Why do you want me to check out some breasts?'

'Why don't you and Billie come over for dinner Friday night and I'll explain everything?'

'Let me check.' I heard Chrissy call out to Billie. 'Yeah, we can do that.'

'Great. See you then.'

* * * * *

Friday's dinner was an event. Chrissy and Billie rolled up with a few bottles of wine and we polished one off before dinner. After dinner, Alex and I came into the lounge to replenished glasses.

'No mucking around with you two,' I said.

'After your question the other night, do you think I'd be sober?' said Chrissy.

I laughed.

'So, whose breasts do you want me to check out?' Chrissy asked.

'Mine.'

Billie froze mid-sip. Unfortunately, Chrissy had taken a sip, promptly started coughing and spat it out all over the coffee table. Alex cleaned up the mess, whilst I went and retrieved my breasts.

'Next time you're going to make a comment like that, make sure I have nothing in my mouth,' Chrissy said when I returned. 'Please, let me restate what I *thought* I heard you say.

'Indeed.' I was smiling. I could see Alex holding the bridge of his nose and shaking his head.

Billie was trying not to laugh. 'This will be good,' she said.

'You be quiet,' scolded Chrissy. 'Now, my dear, dear Peter, you want me to check out *your* breasts?'

'That's right.'

'Don't you mean your chest or nipples?'

'No, my breasts,' I replied. 'These ones,' I added pulling the two bundles from the bag.

I laid them on the table and Billie laughed so hard she cried. 'I wish I had a camera for this.'

'Ssshhh,' said Alex and pointed to the corner of the room where he'd set up his video recorder and had been taping the whole evening.

'You rat!' said Chrissy.

'All for posterity's sake my dear,' countered Alex.

'Forget the camera, we have breasts to deal with,' I said bringing everyone's attention back to the two bundles on the coffee table. 'Alex already knows, I'm creating a drag queen.'

'You are?' Billie exclaimed excitedly.

'I am. For the time being, it's strictly confidential.'

'We'll keep it safe,' said Billie.

'Chrissy?' I asked.

'She'll be fine,' said Billie.

'Here, feel them.' I picked up the breasts and handed one each to Chrissy and Billie.

Chrissy handled it gingerly, as if it was going to explode or something.

Billie however, twisted, turned, squeezed and rolled the breast she had. 'Feels great. Wish mine were this firm and pliable.'

Chrissy shot a look at Billie.

'Lighten up, Chrissy. You've known these boys far too long to be this prudish.'

'Even so, it's not every day I'm asked to feel a breast that's not attached to a body,' Chrissy said.

I filled the glasses. 'Here's to new experiences,' I toasted.

'Here, here,' said Billie.

Alex and Chrissy raised their glasses.

After a few more drinks, Chrissy loosened up and got into rolling the breast around in her hand. 'What's it made of?' she asked.

'That's when the fun began,' I said.

'Why? What do you mean?'

'I started with a combination of washed and cooked rice, raw rice and olive oil. That didn't work.'

'Sounds like it should've.'

'Nah, so I removed the raw rice, as it was feeling too rough. That still didn't work. I was happy with the cooked rice and the oil but it needed more.'

'What did you use?'

'Everything by the looks of the kitchen when I went in,' said Alex. He ducked in time as a cushion was thrown across the room, in his general direction.

'Anyway, I needed something to make it thicker, so I stood and looked at the pantry. I looked at the corn flour and threw in a few teaspoons. Guess what, it worked. Woohoo.'

Everyone laughed.

'An interesting combo. Does the stocking help? What's the goo actually in?' inquired Billie.

'Goo! How rude! It works well, thank you very much. The stocking adds texture and the rice is inside a tough-skinned balloon.'

'Won't they go off?' asked Chrissy.

'Hmm. I hadn't thought of that. I'd better make sure the packages are air-tight then.' I scratched my chin. 'Perhaps I should use an extra balloon?'

'You wouldn't want them leaking either.'

'What a lovely feeling. Oily, claggy old cooked rice dribbling down the inside of my costume.'

'Did you have to be that graphic?' asked Chrissy.

'You asked. I'd heard about using birdseed, although it didn't feel right to me when I tried it. I came upon the rice the one night when Alex brought some Thai sticky rice home for dinner.

'I really hate it when he plays with his food,' Alex chimed in.

'Pffft,' I said. 'I took a spoonful and began to roll it around in my hand.'

'Haven't you done that with rice before?' asked Chrissy.

'Lots of times but you know how sometimes something

you've done so many times before can take on new meaning when your thoughts are in a different place?'

'And that's what happened with you?' asked Billie.

'The rice supply has never been the same since,' said Alex.

'What do you think?' I asked, nodding at the breast in the girl's hands.

'They're actually quite good,' responded Chrissy. 'Yeah, I wish Billie's were like this.'

'Eeeuuuwww. Too much information,' I cried.

The girls laughed.

'They'll look real enough then?' I asked.

'Yeah, they will,' replied Chrissy.

'Why don't you get prosthetics made?' suggested Billie.

'I didn't think they were available in this country yet? Something else to investigate.'

'Nah, leave that to me,' said Billie.

'Oh? Do you know someone, Billie?' I was intrigued.

'Yeah, my brother, Rob, works in the field. I'll see if he can help you.'

'Do you think he would?'

'I'll let you know.'

'Fantastic. Thanks, Billie. Now, that wasn't so hard was it?'

'Not after a few drinks.' Chrissy giggled.

'When's the big unveiling?' asked Billie.

'Not sure yet but when she's ready you'll know.'

'You do realise that I never agreed to be married to a woman,' stated Alex.

'Be quiet,' I said. 'You'll love it.'

We finished off the wine. To be more correct, the girls finished off more of the wine than Alex and I did. We called a cab, as none of us was in a fit state to drive. Alex was propped up against the front porch post as I helped Chrissy and Billie weave their way down the short path. I bundled them into the cab and gave the driver directions. I waved after them as the cab pulled away.

* * * * *

'Hi, Peter.'

'Billie, how you doing tonight?'

'Better now. Wasn't so good Saturday morning.'

'Really?' I tried to sound surprised.

'Anyhoo, I spoke to Rob yesterday …'

'… and?'

'He does make breasts.'

'Can you send me the details?'

'I'll email them later.'

'Great. I'll give him a call and see what happens.'

'At least this way you won't have to deal with breasts that go off.'

'I'm sure I would've discovered that one soon enough.'

'Oh, one more thing?'

'What's up?'

'I may need some help buying a bra.'

Billie laughed. 'Why don't you wait until after you've chatted to Rob? He'll be able to advise on size and shape. Once you know that, then you'll be able to get correctly fitted bras.'

'I hadn't thought of that.'

'No, I'm sure you hadn't.'

'Thanks. Cheers, sweetie.'

5. The Birth of a Lady.

During the 'birthing' process, I'm sure Alex felt like the neglected partner. The spare room downstairs was quickly looking like the op shops I'd been to. Even the old piano was covered with dresses, pants, jackets, boas, shirts. I'd even gone out and bought several foam heads, upon which now sat a variety of wigs. Blonde ones, Red ones, black ones. Some with straight hair. Some with curls. Another teased into a beehive.

'How, and in what scenario, am I ever going to wear that one?' I commented as I sat down to eat dinner one night.

'Wear what, Peter?' asked Alex.

'One of the wigs I bought last week,' I replied. 'I've really only just looked at it.'

'Why did you buy it then?'

'Because I had to.'

'Because you *had* to?'

'Uh-huh,' I muffled through my mouthful of mashed potato and veg. I looked up to see Alex shaking his head and smiling wryly. 'I couldn't pass up a teased beehive, could I?' I added when my mouth was empty.

'Perhaps you should try.'

'As if.' I raced out of the kitchen and returned just as quickly. 'Here, look,' I said, placing the multi-coloured beehive wig on the table.

'I so wish you had have passed that one up,' he declared. 'I don't even know how or where you could wear that one.'

'Ooh, ooh, I know,' I said excitedly.

'Do I really want to know this?' replied Alex.

'Of course you do, my sweet.'

Alex smiled broadly and said happily, 'Tell me, Peter, where are you going to use that wig?'

'When I do my Dusty Wintermeadow impersonation.'

Alex shook his head. 'I told you I didn't want to know.'

'It is delicious though.'

I spent my weeknights playing with options. What wig or shoes went with which dress. There were also the stockings and make-up. Thankfully, I had pages of hints and tips from Karl, the man behind Peachy. Having done theatre before, practising my make-up was relatively easy but Karl's tips were still handy. I'd never actually made myself up to look like a woman when I did theatre. Oh, I had some crazy make-up at times, but never a woman. It's one thing to be bald and have fine swirly patterns painted on your head, it's another to learn how to block out natural eyebrows – and I wasn't about to shave them. The art became how to paint the new ones on a little higher and darker on my forehead. This, of course, gave me more space to add colour and glam to my already stunning eyes.

* * * * *

Having received the email from Billie with her brother's details, I finally got around to calling him. 'Hi, this is Peter Long-Smith, can I speak with Robert Liu please?'

'I'm Rob Liu, how can I help you, Peter?'

'I'm a friend of your sister, Billie, she may have mentioned me?'

'Ah, yes, Peter. You're creating a drag queen or something.'

'Yes I am but I'm keeping it as quiet as I can for now.'

'I understand. How can *I* help you?'

'Did Billie say anything about what I might be asking?'

'Not really, only that she was referring a friend of hers to me.'

'Let me explain then,' I said. 'As you know, I'm creating a drag queen, and I wanted to have a pair of breasts that I could use. I'd worked out something and so invited Billie and her partner, Chrissy, over for dinner for an assessment.'

'Yes, Billie did mention something about that.'

I laughed. 'It was a fun night. I don't think one drop of the four bottles of wine they brought with them, was left.'

'That sounds like Billie.' Rob laughed.

'After they'd finished playing with my breasts, Billie suggested you.'

'I see. How can I help you?'

'I'd like you to make me a pair. Can you do it?' I asked simply.

'That shouldn't be a problem. When do you need them by?'

'How quickly can you make them?'

'Once I get the size you want, it should only take about a week to craft.'

'I can live with that.'

'Did Billie give you my email details as well?'

'Yeah, she did.'

'Send me the size you want, your basic details – as in height and weight. How you intend to wear them and any other information you think might be relevant.'

'I'll get that off for you as soon as I can.'

* * * * *

Over the next week, I discovered the voice I wanted to use. This then led me to the name. One thing led to another and the combination of the voice and the name helped me decide the look I'd use for the 'birth' of my new alter ego.

The only costume I bought from a costume store needed

some work. The frill on the arms and hemline needed replacing but that was easy to deal with. I also decided to remove all the hoops except the bottom one but after trying it on and walking around, it too was removed. After I'd finished with the needlework and touch-ups, I had it dry-cleaned and it came back looking alive. In all my travels for costumes, fabrics, and so on, I came across a hair spray that was infused with glitter. I successfully used it on some sample fabrics and some of the wigs and so I decided to put a light coat over the dress I was going to wear for the birth. I hung the dress up and began to work. After about thirty minutes, I stepped back and reviewed my work.

'Yes, very nice indeed.'

I was ready.

'She's ready dear,' I announced over dinner one Friday night.

'Who is?' Alex replied.

I looked at him curiously. 'You trying to block her out already?' I said. 'Nice.'

Alex chuckled.

'I want you home tomorrow night,' I stated.

'Indeed. What if I had something else planned?'

'Without me? I don't think so.'

'I might have,' replied Alex. 'As it happens, I don't, so I will be at home tomorrow night.'

'That's better.'

'I'm looking forward to it.'

* * * * *

After dinner, it took me about an hour to get ready, though it felt longer. I was so nervous. Fully costumed, I manoeuvred through the kitchen to the dining room. I pressed play on the stereo I'd set earlier. I daresay Alex jumped when the music started. The house had been relatively silent once dinner was finished.

I took a deep breath and stepped through the curtains hanging in the doorway between the lounge and dining rooms.

'Daaarlings, my name is Madame Prissy DuPonce,' I said in the masculine, yet slightly high-pitched voice I had decided to use. 'But you can call me Prissy.'

For her debut, Prissy appeared as a southern belle. The skirt was pastel pink satin, with its light shimmer of glitter. A white frill graced the hem. The bodice was also made of pink satin and had a white ruffle around the neck and down the centre where it buttoned. The long sleeves were puffed from shoulder to elbow, where a frill separated it from the rest of the sleeve. The sleeve from the elbow to wrist was more fitted and was finished at the cuff with yet another piece of frilly lace. The blonde wig was styled high, with fine ringlets hanging beside the ears. A small pink doll-sized whimsy was pinned on top of the wig. The parasol was a darker shade of pink than the dress and was covered in a thin layer of white lace.

'I'm here to give you your weekly dose of trash, gossip and song. Sit back, relax, and enjoy the show.'

I pressed the remote once more and skipped the music to the performance song. When that concluded, I swept back through the curtains to the dining room and turned the music off.

I can't remember if the camera flashed or not, I was too busy remembering my character, moves and the words for the song. Still, I heard nothing from the other side of the curtain, so I poked my head through to find that Alex wasn't moving. Standing before him, still dressed, I poked him gently with the tip of the parasol. This brought a reaction. He jumped, dropped the camera on the couch and spilt some of the wine.

Alex calmed and then couldn't stop smiling. 'That was fantastic. I loved it. I want to see more.'

'You think so?'

'Oh my god, yyyeeessss. She'll be a smash hit from day

one, of that I'm sure.'

'You have to say that, sweetie.'

'I mean it. Tell me otherwise after her debut at RPs.'

'We'll see.'

'Trust me.'

'I do,' I said. 'Now I'm nervous.'

'That's good, isn't it?'

'In theatre, yes.'

'Then what are you worrying about?'

'More than I probably should.'

'Well I loved it.'

'I'm glad you do, sweetie. I'd love to stay and chat but I have other places to visit.'

Prissy vanished as quickly as she had arrived.

About forty-five mins later, I returned to the lounge, and a beaming Alex.

Alex handed me a glass of champagne. 'That was amazing.' He was still excited.

'You really think so?' I repeated.

'Yes. Wait 'til the boys at RPs get a load of her.'

'I hope they like her too.'

'Are you going to be like the female performer they have at RPs who rewrites the words? I know you said you were going to do a combination of live and mime.'

'I haven't thought that far ahead but I might.' I replied.

'When's the work do?'

'Early December.'

'Plenty of time, it's only August.'

'I know,' I replied. 'I have to gather a bunch of songs first.'

'Let me know what you're looking for and I'll see what I can dig up,' offered Alex.

'Thanks, hon. I'll let you know,' I said. 'I don't think Prissy will debut as she did tonight though for RPs.'

'Why not? The costume looked fine?'

'I'll think about it some more,' I said. 'At least I get to have fun shopping.'

'Haven't you got enough yet?'

'Probably not.' I chuckled.

'What about having some costumes made?'

'Who would do that?'

'I reckon Terese might be interested.'

'Your sister?'

'Yeah,' said Alex. 'She is a dressmaker after all.'

'Would she want to be made famous by a drag queen?'

'Only one way to find out.'

Alex grabbed the phone and started dialling.

'Who are you calling at this time?' I asked

'Ssshhh,' was all I got in reply. 'Hey, sis,' said Alex. '... Did I get you out of bed or something?'

I began to wave like a woman possessed.

'Hang on a minute ...,' said Alex and turned towards me. 'Stop having a hissy-fit like a spoilt child. It's the only way we'll know. Perhaps I should start calling it a Prissy-fit'

'Very funny,' I replied sarcastically. I folded into the chair.

'I'm back. Are you going to be home tomorrow? ... Peter has a proposition for you.'

'No I don't!' Alas, my plea was in vain.

'Here he is.'

Alex tried to hand me the phone but I refused.

He insisted.

I refused.

He thrust the phone at me once more so that I had to grab it if only to stop it from crashing into my face.

'Now talk!' he said sternly.

I sighed heavily.

'Hey, Terese.'

'Peter, darling, how are you?'

'Exhausted.'

'Oh? What have you been doing to my Alex?'

'Oh please, nothing like that. Not that I'd ever admit

anything like that to you anyway. Eeuuww!'

Terese laughed. I had to join her.

'Now, what have you done that has Alex calling me at ten o'clock at night?'

'I gave birth to a drag queen tonight.'

'You did what?'

'I gave birth to a drag queen tonight.'

'And a damned good one too,' Alex added leaning into the phone. I pushed him away.

'Intriguing. Why does he have you talking to me?'

'He thinks you might be interested in making some costumes for me?'

Even Alex jumped at the squeal from the phone. Alex mouthed *I told you so.*

I waved an unkind hand gesture in his direction. He left the room laughing.

'I take it that means yes?'

'You betcha it does sweetie. I love my craft and I've always wanted to do theatre. My Jeremy has just about had enough of me getting involved with his school productions these past couple of years.'

'I guess we can talk about it tomorrow.'

'Indeed we will. Bring anything with you that you already have and we can start from there.'

'Okay. See you tomorrow.'

'Come for lunch. Eleven-thirty okay?'

'We'll be there,' said Alex.

I didn't even hear him pick up the other handset.

'See ya, boys.'

Alex came back into the lounge room.

'You bastard!'

'You love me for it.'

I uttered a low growl. Alex came and hugged me. How could I stay angry with him? 'Thanks,' I said, kissing him on the cheek.

'All you needed was a push.'

'She's in motion now. She'll either crash and burn very quickly or she'll roar through town leaving gaping mouths in her wake.'

'The latter I hope.'

'We'll see.'

'So is Prissy going to the work function then?'

'Yeah, except I'm not telling anyone who's behind her. Well not just yet.'

'You'll need a minder slash manager.'

'Minder yes, though I'll probably act as 'manager' as Prissy is only going to be a stage drag queen.'

'Pardon?'

'Performance only,' I explained. 'She won't arrive in drag, if it can be avoided, and hopefully not too many will know.'

'Ah,' replied Alex. 'Keeping it a secret won't be easy.'

'I know.'

* * * * *

With Prissy's debut at home before Alex, I decided to ring Karl and give him the good news.

'Karl, Peter here. Did you have a good weekend?' I said on Monday night after Prissy's debut.

'Hey, Peter. It was busy as usual. We had a big night at RPs Saturday. We didn't see you or Alex there. Things okay?'

'They're fine thanks. We had an event of our own Saturday night.'

'I trust it's all good?'

'Yes it is. Madame Prissy DuPonce was brought into the world.'

'Prissy who?'

'Prissy DuPonce. My drag queen.'

'Ah, yes. Congratulations.'

'Thanks,' I said.

'I'm not even going to ask where you got the name from.'

I laughed.

'When did you want to debut her to the public?' asked Karl.

'I was thinking later this month?'

'Let me grab the diary.'

I reached for mine.

'How does the ... first Saturday in September sound?'

'Looks good to me.'

'Done. I'll advertise the fact from the stage a couple of weeks leading up to the night.'

'I can cope with that.'

'Great. I'm looking forward to it.'

'Just have a case of booze ready for me before the show.'

Karl laughed heartily. 'You'll be fine. You'll be too nervous to drink. I'll have something there for you all the same.'

6. Couture 101.

'Can you come over tomorrow arvo for a body glove fitting?'

'You work fast.' I was surprised to get her call a week after our first conversation. Terese, Alex's dressmaker sister, enthusiastically came on board as my official seamstress.

'Your body glove was easy. I had to make one for one of Jeremy's classmates. They needed a tall female and as none of the girls in his school were tall enough, one of the boys agreed to do it.'

'Yeah, I can come over tomorrow.'

'Wonderful. See you then.'

*****

As soon as I walked in to her work bungalow, Terese handed me a bundle of fabric and latex. I unfolded it and held it before me.

'Your new body glove dear.'

'Interesting.' I began to feel every part of it. The latex chest. The hidden zipper down the back. I found a couple of pouches sewn inside. 'Pouches?'

'Yeah. In case you need to replace the breasts at any stage, and so you can swap between the sleeveless, short-sleeve and long-sleeve body gloves.' She indicated two other bundles on a side table.

'Ah yes. I'll probably use the sleeveless one the most. Can you make another?'

'Sure.'

'What's with the latex chest though?'

'Now you have a very real looking cleavage.'

'Wow.' I fished around in my backpack and inserted the prosthetic breasts Rob had made for me. Terese had also successfully made arrangements to tuck away that-which-determined-who-I-was (which wasn't an easy feat). I would not have thought of using a cricket cup! I ducked behind a screen she'd set up and after climbing into my new body glove, my hairy legs sticking out the bottom, some tweaking was required. She measured waist, hips and breasts, which was the most unusual.

'Will you stop laughing so I can get the measurements,' said Terese tersely.

'It's hard,' I replied, still chuckling. 'It's not often I stand in a woman's sewing room wearing nothing other than a body hugging outfit that has breasts.'

'This is a first for me too,' she replied.

'No it's not.'

'Huh?' Terese was bewildered.

'Like you said, you'd made one of these for one of Jeremy's classmates.'

'Oh yeah, I did too. Still, no excuse for you to fidget.'

'Ow!' I cried, rubbing a spot on my leg. 'Why'd you go and do that for?'

'I'm sorry, the pin must've slipped.'

'Suuure it did.' I continued to rub my leg. I looked up to see Alex sniggering. 'It's not funny.'

'Yes it is,' he said, now chuckling. I saw him fishing around in his pockets. Withdrawing his hand, I saw the enemy of all enemies. 'Say cheese.'

'Don't you dare...'

'Too late.'

'You'll keep.'

'Oooh, I'm sooo scared now.' Alex feigned being scared, waved a dismissive hand in my direction and continued taking photos.

'Be warned,' I said. I jerked my leg at the sudden rush of pain. 'What the f.....!'

'If you don't stand still, I'll rip out more than a few,' scolded Terese, holding up a few of the hairs from my leg.

She finally got the measurements she wanted.

'Now, do you want your costumes to fit snugly or not?'

'To a degree,' I replied.

Terese looked at me.

'I want them to look snug but I'll need room to move as I perform,' I explained. 'I also don't want them to look like balloons. I know I don't have a size 00 figure ...'

'... That's true,' interrupted Alex.

I ignored the comment. '... but I'm not huge either. To quote the famous Lola Fla-nel, it should be tight enough to show I'm a woman and loose enough to show I'm a lady.'

Alex just laughed.

'You'll look stunning my dear,' replied Terese.

'I hope so.'

'What do you want?'

'Pardon?'

'What styles, colours, and cut do you want?'

'Ah. Surprise me. Give me four options, if that's not too much.'

'Not at all.'

'I know, what about this: Las Vegas showgirl meets grandma at a wedding?' I added.

Even Alex looked at me oddly this time. 'Las Vegas showgirl meets grandma at a wedding – what the hell is that?' he said.

'I think I know what he means, Al,' replied Terese. 'Leave it to me.'

‘See, like she said,’ I said, taunting Alex.

* * * * *

Whilst I waited for Terese to do the costumes, I concentrated on the music, choosing four songs for that first night. I knew I’d only need two but as the motto goes ‘Be Prepared’. I’d seen acts appear on stage, do their allotted numbers then have no back up when the crowd wanted more.

One song I decided to rewrite and perform live. I purchased the rights to use the backing track and contacted friends in the music industry who helped me jazz it up a little and add some backing vocals, which I recorded.

Once the track was finished, I performed it for Alex at home.

‘What on earth possessed you to use that song?’ he asked after I’d finished. ‘I didn’t think Junee Andrews was that much of a gay icon.’

‘She’s not,’ I said. ‘Do you think I’d pass up such a good song though?’

‘Not at all.’

We were so excited about how well it worked, that we rewrote one of the other songs. We were almost in tears when it was done. When my friends had finished rearranging the music for that song, I performed it at their studio for them.

So there it was, by the middle of August I had four songs ready to go. Two I would mime and two I would sing live. I chose the two that would be the official performance songs and made sure the cues were right.

* * * * *

‘What do you mean they’re done?’ I asked incredulously, speaking to Terese a week later.

‘They’re done,’ Terese repeated.

'I don't know what to say?'

'Save it for the viewing,' she said. 'Come around after lunch and have a look. I need to make sure they fit.'

'We'll be there.'

I walked into Terese's bungalow and was stunned.

'What do you think?' asked Terese.

'I don't know what to say.'

'That's a first,' added Alex.

'Scrag.'

'Trollop.'

'Okay you two,' scolded Terese.

Draped on dressmaker's dummies were four of the most stunning costumes I'd ever seen. The first was a royal blue satin and sequined dress that was a trimmed version of the southern belle costume I'd used to present Prissy to Alex. Terese had even made a hat and parasol to match in pale blue silk.

'I know exactly which wig to wear with the blue one,' I indicated.

The second was a pale green midi skirt with yellow tulle petticoats. A jade green, tailed jacket and white frilly shirt complemented the skirt.

'Hmmm, cabaret-cum-Ms. Milder.' I mused aloud. 'Yes, I know where I can wear that one.'

The next one along was a long white chiffon coat over an orange dress. Small sequins and white faux pearls decorated the fitted bodice.

The fourth costume was a black tailored suit with a knee-length skirt and matching jacket. Terese had presented it with a lilac silk shirt and purple silk tie.

'Daaarlink, they're gorgeous,' I said with Prissy's voice. 'I'll take all four.'

'I thought you only wanted two!' stated Terese.

'For the show at RPs darling, I do,' I replied. 'I need something for my work's Christmas function. That's where I'll wear the black suit.'

'So you're happy?'

'Sweetie darling, I'm very happy.' Wrapping Terese in a huge hug, I sloppily kissed her on the cheek.

'Yes!' Terese dragged her fist down through the air triumphantly, once I had released her from the hug. 'Does this mean I get to make more?'

'I wouldn't dream of using anyone else.'

'Hello.' Alex tried butting in.

'The blue one will be great for my first performance at RPs.'

'I look forward to seeing it in action.'

'Don't worry, you'll be there.'

'Great.'

'HELLO.'

'Then I'll use the green one for the second show that night,' I continued.

'HELLO!'

'Will you be quiet, Alex!' Terese turned to her younger brother.

'Whose idea was this?' he asked.

'Yes, sweetie, I know it was your idea to ask your sister,' I said, giving him a huge hug and a kiss.

'Thank you,' he replied, uncrossing his arms.

'What will you use the white one for?' asked Terese.

'I'm not sure yet,' I replied, stroking my chin. 'There'll be chances to wear it.'

'If you look closely,' said Terese moving towards the models, 'I've designed a couple of them so they can be mixed and matched.'

'Excellent,' I said. 'That will help. Ooh, ooh, ooh ...'

'What sweetie?' asked Terese.

'I know where I can wear the white one?'

'Where's that, hon?' asked Alex.

'When I'm presented with next year's Queen's Honours

award for most outstanding new talent!'

Terese laughed. Alex groaned.

I turned to see Alex fishing in his pockets again.

'What've you lost?' I asked him.

'I was checking to see if I'd brought your medication or not.'

'What?'

'For your delusions of grandeur. The doctor warned me this could happen.'

'Oh, very funny.'

This time Alex laughed along with Terese. He came over and gave me a hug.

'They do look good.'

'They certainly do.'

'Well, try them on,' urged Alex, waving his hands at me.

I tried each one on in turn. The only thing missing were the shoes and wigs. Terese gave me some fabric samples to take shopping.

'I've made them about two sizes larger than you need, even with the body glove on,' explained Terese as she helped me slip into the costumes.

'Smart girl,' I said.

'That way, you can get in and out of them quickly. You can then bring them in with the hidden ties inside.'

'Hmmm, so that's where all the smarts went.'

I heard the distinct 'harrumph' from the corner of the room.

'I still love you, dear,' I called to Alex.

'Just as well.'

After three hours of changing, pinning, and fitting, Alex and I left.

'I'll come over the night before to finalise the two I want for RPs,' I said.

'When's that?'

'Two weeks.'

'Can you come over again next week?'

'I should be able to. I'll let you know if I can't. Why?'

'I want to make sure these alterations are okay.'

'Fair enough. See you then.'

'Sounds great,' replied Terese.

'Make sure you write the bill out fully,' I said. 'Whilst I'm happy for family to help me out, I also like to pay for what I get.'

'I will.'

'Mind you, if it's too outrageous, I will say something,' I added, smiling.

Armed with the fabric samples, I went hunting for more shoes. The wigs I already had would work well with the costumes, so I was happy with those choices. Whilst I had several pairs of shoes already, a girl can never have too many.

'Not more shoes,' whined Alex when I arrived home with another box.

'I think I've got enough now,' I replied.

'We'll need a new house soon.'

'Perhaps we do. A room for Prissy at least.'

'I was joking,' said Alex, bewildered.

I was lost in thought. 'Not this year though.'

7. Prissy's First Gig.

The two frocks I'd chosen for the shows at RPs were now hanging in their bags downstairs. I woke on the first Saturday in September, too early for my liking. Rather than sit around home waiting, I went to the gym after having a light breakfast. I was so nervous, I worked out for about two hours. I came home to Alex having a shower.

'Leave it on,' I called into the bathroom. We passed in the hall and I stood and soaked my aching muscles in the warmth of the water.

Alex was reading the paper and having a coffee when I came downstairs. 'You want to have lunch at the Buckingham today?' he asked.

'Yeah, let someone else do the running around.'

When we got home, Alex left me alone as I fussed over costumes, wigs, shoes and make-up. I must've gone up and down the stairs a hundred times that afternoon.

'First a new house and now it looks like we'll need new carpet on the stairs,' commented Alex at one stage.

'What did you say?' I said, not particularly listening.

'Never mind.' Alex smiled and shook his head.

I finally stopped at about five and sat on the couch. Alex came up behind me and massaged my shoulders. I hadn't realised he'd stopped until I woke. 'What time is it?' I asked sleepily.

'Six-thirty.'

I sat bolt upright. 'It can't be that late.'

'Yes it can.'

'You should've woken me.'

'You needed the rest.'

'Now I'll be late.'

'No you won't,' said Alex. 'You don't have to be at RPs until nine at the earliest. The first show isn't until ten-thirty. Relax.'

I started to pace, then began fussing over the costumes again. Alex was the calm one that day. I can look back now and laugh. I was in such a state after the nap that I must've looked half-crazed.

Alex stopped me gently in my tracks. 'Sweetie,' he said looking into my eyes, 'I've run you a bath with some oils and essences. I *do not* want to see you for at least thirty minutes. Understand?'

'I have stuff to do.'

'Understand?' He said it so firmly, yet gently, that it caught me off guard.

'I understand,' I said bowing my head.

I trudged upstairs and entered the bathroom. Not only had he run the bath, some of my favourite relaxation music was playing and there was a glass of champagne.

'What have I done to deserve all this?' I mused to myself.

I slipped into the bath and closed my eyes. I didn't hear Alex come in until he coughed gently. I jumped a little. 'When did you come in?'

'About five minutes ago.'

'Why didn't you wake me, again?'

'You looked at peace.'

'I do feel better.'

'Good. I have a snack prepared.'

'I had better get out and get dressed.'

'Indeed. I don't want to eat my dinner looking at a naked you.'

'Pffft.'

Alex leaned over and kissed me. 'See you downstairs.'

He'd prepared some steamed vegetables and as we sat and ate, he raised a toast to a successful evening.

Although I knew the dressing rooms were upstairs, I still asked for directions when we arrived just after nine. I was the first performer to arrive. Peachy had cleared a space on one wall, where she'd hung a large glittery, star-shaped nametag emblazoned with Prissy.

'It's really happening?' I said staring at the name hanging on the hook.

'Yes it is, Pete.' Alex hung the costume bag he had on one of the hooks.

I hung the other one and placed the make-up bag on the table next to it. We came back downstairs and had a drink. I went to the bathroom several times before I saw Karl arrive. I followed him upstairs.

'Nervous?' he asked.

'Very,' I replied.

'Then you'll do well.'

'I hope so.'

'My advice is simply to relax and enjoy the moment. Don't worry about what the crowd says or does. You've been here, you know what they're like.'

'That I do.'

Karl began to apply his make-up; I sat down and did the same. I was about halfway through when the other act, Dinah Soare, arrived. She already had her make-up on and she wished me well. By ten-fifteen I had become Prissy. Alex came upstairs just as I was finished.

'Hi Peachy, is Pete here?' he asked.

'I saw him earlier, then he vanished,' replied Peachy.

'Okay thanks.' Alex began to leave.

I coughed delicately. Alex turned and smiled.

'Hi, sweetie,' he said. 'You look great.'

'You think so?'

'Yes I do,' said Alex. 'Doesn't she girls?'

Peachy and Dinah both agreed that Prissy looked fabulous.

'With the make-up you've done, no one will know who you are,' Peachy said.

'That's good to know,' I said. 'I want it to be that way for a while.'

'I had better go and announce the first show.' Peachy left the room.

I took a sharp breath and turned to Alex.

He reached over and caressed my face gently. 'Relax and enjoy yourself. You know the words. You know the moves. You know the character. Now go and show them who's Madam.'

I kissed Alex. 'I love you so much.'

'I love you too.'

Peachy returned. 'Time to go girls.'

Peachy led us downstairs and we hovered in the back room waiting our turn to perform. I saw Alex disappear to the main room to sit with friends. Ten-thirty arrived. Peachy did her opening number. The crowd loved her, as they always do. I could hear Peachy doing her announcements, bad gags and gossip. Then I heard that she was introducing a new act. My heart skipped several beats. I began to flap my hands over my face. I could feel my temperature rising.

I quickly looked to my right when I felt a touch on my arm.

'Relax and enjoy yourself dear. Chookas, as they say,' encouraged Dinah, patting my arm a few times. I placed my hand over hers and smiled.

'Is she up my chute yet?'

That was my cue. I walked along the hall. Peachy was still on stage. As I stood there, I rubbed my hands over each other repeatedly, waiting. Waiting. Waiting. Suddenly it hit me. *My name was just announced.* I took several quick breaths to try to calm myself. Smoothed my dress. Ran my hand gently over my wig. I began looking around for a shiny surface to check my make-up. I spotted the large mirror on the wall in the back lounge, although I only had time to smile and make sure there was no lippy on my teeth - or spinach. My music started. The crowd was polite with their applause as I stepped on stage.

I bustled past a couple of guys right by the stage and gracefully climbed the two steps to the top. I gazed out over the sea of faces. Some turned to their neighbours and yabbered about who knows what. *I wonder what they're thinking. Who's this up-start, probably? She doesn't look anything special.* The ceiling fans were rippling the rainbow coloured banners hanging from the roof. I saw Peachy watching from the end of the bar. It was different being on stage. I was used to being in the dark, watching others on the semi-spot lit stage. Now it was my turn to be under those same lights.

For this very first time on stage, I had chosen to sing one of my rewritten songs. The intro swelled and I started.

Mascarared lashes, so long and so flashy
Lips of bright colour, you'd think I was trashy.
I am an angel with silvery wings,
I am a diva with plenty of bling.

Over the music and the incessantly loud beating of my own heart, I could hear the crowd laughing and occasionally cheering. I watched a few faces in the front couple of rows grimace slightly at the choice of song I'd chosen to rewrite.

Boys in tight blue jeans with smooth and tanned faces,
Muscular chests tied with leathery braces,
Tattoos are tribal and platinum rings
These are a few of my favourite things.

However, they changed when I teased them during the second verse. I continued to sing the next few verses and chorus and move about the stage. With the song I'd chosen, it was easy to extend it and make it a little more interesting. I spotted Alex in the crowd smiling proudly. I saw someone lean in to him and he shook his head. I realised I was coming to the end of the song and as I did a spin, I caught my reflected image in the large mirror hanging at the back of the stage. The blue of the dress, the sequins twinkling made me slightly teary. *I can't believe this is going so well.* I gave it everything I had.

When the plans hatch, when the claws scratch
When the drags are mad
I simply remember how special I am,
And then I don't feel so bad.

Even as I was finishing, the crowd was going ballistic.

Peachy came on stage. 'What do you think boys?'

The crowd cheered.

'Encore.'

'We want more.'

'Show us what you've got!'

'You'll get more, Prissy DuPonce will be returning for the second show.'

I left the stage to wild applause and I heard Dinah being announced. I felt for Dinah. Having to perform for a crowd in that state. Afterwards, I mentioned it to her and she was pleased as the crowd seemed to enjoy her song all the more and it spurred her on.

'That was fantastic,' said a dark haired boy, stopping me as I moved through the back room.

'Thank you, sweetie. You're too kind,' I gushed. I planted a huge red kiss on his cheek, much to the delight of his friends.

'I want a photo,' called another, stopping me again. I leaned in to him, put my lips on his cheeks and waited for the flash. 'Thanks, Madam.'

'Bring it back one day and I'll autograph it for you.' I laughed as I walked through the door and up the stairs.

Once inside the peace and quiet of the changing room, I flopped into a chair. I jumped when Alex entered the room.

'Did you see that?' he said. His smile was bigger than I'd ever seen.

'I did. I can't believe it,' I replied. We hugged tightly.

We parted when Peachy and Dinah came into the room. Alex left.

'That was amazing,' said Dinah.

'Thank you,' I replied.

'I'm impressed,' said Peachy. 'The crowd loved it.'

I began to blush. 'You think so?'

'Excuse me! Does a gay man stand when they play 'God Save the Queen', declaring loudly that she's arrived?' Peachy's arms outstretched, palms open.

I smiled and Peachy saw the tear in my eye.

'You should be happy, my dear, and proud. You're a natural. Utterly, utterly faaaabulous.'

'I'll work with you anytime,' added Dinah.

'Thanks, ladies.'

The second show came and the crowd called for Prissy as soon as Peachy stepped on stage.

'Keep ya jocks on boys,' said Peachy. 'Madame DuPonce will return shortly.'

The crowd cheered. I was to perform last in the second show and I decided to sing the other rewritten song. I advised the soundman of the new cue and we were set.

'To close the show tonight, and not for the last time,' announced Peachy after her song, 'I give you Madame Prissy DuPonce.'

8. Prissy Something

It was early September, and you'd think things would be quiet. Spring had only just begun. The weather was going to get warmer, we hoped. Moreover, Christmas was still almost four months away. How wrong I was.

From here on, various events came and went. Some in very quick succession. Some filling a few weeks at a time. Either way, there was no, or very little, rest for me. What with the birth of a drag queen, followed by ... nah, you'll have to wait and read them as they happened. Then you'll understand how it was.

I guess it began pretty much the weekend I debuted at RPs. The response was far beyond my wildest dreams. At least I knew the character I'd created would be well received. All I had to do now was get ready for the staff function, see how that went and then canvas options for the following year, if I felt confident enough to do it again.

Being very excited, Alex and I stayed at RPs for drinks after the last show. I was far too wound up to sleep. Alex went to bed about two and I crawled in a couple of hours later. By the time I saw anything of Sunday, it was late afternoon. For the rest of the day, I simply lounged around the house. My productivity wasn't all that crash hot at work on Monday. Thankfully, Alex sensed how I was feeling when I came home and did everything for dinner that evening.

'I'll get it,' I said patting Alex's knee as I rose to answer the phone. 'You've done a lot tonight and I thank you for it.' I kissed his forehead as I moved away from the couch.

I picked up the phone. 'Hello? ... Hey, Karl.'

'How did you pull up after Saturday night?'

'Better than I thought.'

'Good. I have a proposition for you?'

'Ah-ha?'

'I want you to join me on stage, on a regular basis. You interested?'

I hoped I curbed my enthusiasm at his proposal. 'I'll have to think about it.'

'Sure. No hurry.'

'Thanks for the offer. I wasn't expecting that.'

'I don't make them lightly.'

'I'm honoured. I'll give you a call in a few days or so.'

'Fantastic.'

I placed the handset in its cradle.

'Who was that?' asked Alex.

'That was Karl offering me, Prissy actually, a regular place on stage.'

'That's great, Pete. What did you say?'

'Nothing yet. I said I'd call him back in a few days.'

'What do you want to say?'

'Yes, of course. This involves two people and I don't mean Prissy this time.'

'Like us not seeing each other as much as we'd like? Like you spending more money on costumes, wigs, shoes and make-up? Like you spending more time working on songs?'

'Yes, like all of those.'

'From the day you told me you were going to create Prissy, I've been planning for one of two eventualities.'

'Oh? And you haven't told me about either of these?'

'Up until this moment, I didn't need to.'

'What are these two eventualities?'

'The first isn't a new direction, just the same as what we've already got.'

'Okay. The second?'

'The second involved you receiving such a response that it became like a second job. I've thought through how much time you'd need to do it all. How little time we're likely to spend with each other.'

'And?'

'I want you to do this.'

'Why?'

'Because I love you. Because you love theatre. I've always known that. I saw how much you enjoyed yourself Saturday night and how fabulously the crowd reacted to you.'

He was standing before me, holding my hands, beaming.

I couldn't hold it in anymore. 'WOOOOOOOOOOOO-FREAKIN'-HOOOOOOOOOOOOOOO' I called out as loud as I could.

Alex laughed and we hugged and bounced around like a pair of giddy schoolgirls. Eventually we calmed down and finished off the bottle of wine from dinner.

'Perhaps I should call Karl tonight?' I said, emptying my glass.

'Give it a few days and make sure.'

'Okay.'

* * * * *

The following night, Alex and I were at the Buckingham Hotel for a trivia night. The Buckingham is a classic suburban hotel. The bar, with its array of sporting memorabilia above it, was the first thing you saw when you entered the main door. Located on a corner, the bar stretched left and right. Stools lined up next to the bar. High tables were scattered about the place and four-seater booths were nestled along the walls. There was a second door that came off the main street, which opened on to a hallway bringing the patron through to a larger, more open room, where the trivia night took place. There was a small stage on the wall closest to the bar. Between the entrance to the bar and the stage, stairs lead to the upper level.

Devon Hawthorne, owner of the Buckingham, came over to speak with us towards the end of the evening. We'd known Devon for a long time and had often been out to dinner or functions with him and his wife.

'Were you guys at RPs last Sat'day night?' he asked.

'I was,' replied Alex. 'Peter wasn't feeling the best and had a quiet one at home.'

I squeezed Alex's hand gently under the table.

'I hope you're feelin' better now, Pete?'

'I am,' I replied. 'I think I was a little over-tired and needed to rest.'

'Why do you want to know if we were at RPs Saturday night?' asked Alex. 'And what were you doing there?' he quizzed further.

'It was our youngest son's birthday and after eating out, he wanted us all to go to his favourite place,' explained Devon. 'It didn't bother Carol or me, although I think some of his siblings felt a little out of place.'

We laughed.

'Ever since then, I've been tryin' to get in contact with one of the performers,' he replied. 'No one knows how to.'

'Oh, which one,' I asked tentatively.

'The new one that Peachy had, Prissy something.'

'You mean Prissy DuPonce?' asked Alex.

'Yeah, her. I even rang RPs this arvo but they didn't have any contact details. I was given Peachy's number, except it goes to voicemail. I've left a message and I guess I'll have ta wait.'

'I see,' I said. 'Why do you want to get in contact with her?'

'I want her to do a show here on a Friday night and also at the Governor on a Thursday night'

'The Governor?' I queried.

'I've been helpin' manage the hotel lately and I reckon Prissy would be great for both places.'

I looked over at Alex who smiled and nodded.

'We can contact Prissy for you,' I said.

'You can?'

'It's quite easy really.'

Devon looked puzzled.

'You have to promise me one thing though Devon?'

'C'mon boys. How long 'ave we known each other? Don't ya trust me? What's up?'

'Promise not to reveal to anyone what I am about to tell you, unless otherwise told by Alex or myself.'

'O … kay.'

'I am Prissy DuPonce.'

'You? Nah, it can't be.'

'Yes it can.'

'Well I never,' said Devon, astounded. He had a closer look at me. 'I can see a vague resemblance.'

'I'll need a few days to think about it though.'

'Take whatever time you need.' We shook on it.

* * * * *

All day at work, my brain had been in a whirl. *Did I really want to be a drag queen full time?* Now that *was* a stupid thought. Of course I did, otherwise I wouldn't have said yes to Devon to consider his offer. It also confirmed my initial decision to say yes to Karl. Once I had resolved that, the rest of my day flew by, even though I had to work back late. Alex was home earlier than I was and had already started dinner.

I breezed through to the kitchen and was obviously unaware of my state of being.

'Well, you're the cat who got the cream,' commented Alex. 'What gives?'

'I made a final decision today.'

'Should I be happy?'

'Yes, you should. I'm going to accept Karl's offer, even though we'd already talked about it on Monday night.'

'Congratulations, sweetie.'

'I can't wait any longer, Alex, I have to call Karl.'

'Are you sure?'

'In a way, you helped me decide last night.' I smiled lovingly at him, leaning against the kitchen bench.

He looked puzzled. 'How did I do that? Last night we were at the Buckingham for a trivia night.'

'Yes we were. Then Devon came and talked to us.'

'And?'

I looked over to you when Devon said he wanted to get in contact with Prissy. You smiled at me and nodded. Initially I took that as a yes to tell him who Prissy was. I also realised, after a fashion, that you were saying yes to the whole thing in general. In effect, by saying yes to Devon, I was saying yes to Karl. After all he did ask first.'

Alex pondered what I said. I watched as his brow knit and un-knit and knit once more. Then he smiled. 'Go call Karl.'

I planted a wet, sloppy raspberry kiss on his cheek.

'Yuck,' he cried, as I left the room.

'You love it.' I laughed. I made the call.

'How's my new star?' asked Karl.

'Saying yes,' I answered. 'I'll at least give it a trial for you.'

'That's great.'

'Thanks. Alex was the one who convinced me.'

'You've got a great man there.'

'I have.'

'How soon can you start?' queried Karl.

'How soon would you like me?'

'Have you got some more songs?'

'I had four prepared and I did three of them on the first night.'

Karl laughed. 'I don't think the boys will mind if you repeat.'

'Possibly. Guess I need to get to work on some more material. I have some options, I just have to clean them up.'

'Why don't you come back next week and then do every second week until the end of the year?'

'That sounds fine for now,' I said. 'I'll mark my diary and if things need to change, I'll let you know.'

'Great.'

'I have one slightly embarrassing question.'

'Fire away.'

'Will I get paid from now on?'

Karl chuckled. 'Yes you will. Why don't you and Alex drop in this week and I can go over some of these things?'

'I have one more request,' I asked.

'What is it?'

'For the time being, I'd prefer to keep my identity a secret. I have to do a work function in December and I don't want my colleagues to know who's behind Prissy yet.'

'That's not a problem at all. At the start we all want our 'Clark Kent' kept secret.'

With the excitement of talking to Karl coursing through my veins, I rang Devon.

'Pete, it's good to ta hear from ya so soon,' said Devon.

'I have good news,' I said. 'I'm saying yes to your proposal.'

'That's great. When can ya start?'

'How about an October start? Second Friday for the Buckingham, and third Thursday for the Gov.?' I suggested.

'I'll need ta get back to ya,' replied Devon. 'Although that sounds fine so far.'

'I do have a slightly odd question.'

'Sure, what is it?'

'what about payment? We are talking about me being paid, aren't we?'

Devon chuckled. 'Course ya will. Why don't you drop in this week so can go over the details?'

'I have one more request,' I asked.

'Sure,'

'For the time being, I'd rather not let people know who I am. I don't want people know who Prissy is just yet.'

'I can do that for ya, Pete,' said Devon.

'What have I agreed to do?' I said, returning to the dining room to have dinner.

'To sign your life away to a drag queen,' Alex calmly replied.

'I see.'

'You sure now?'

'It's all I thought about.'

'Hmmm, so did I.'

'Why?' I looked at Alex.

'I got to thinking about you rehearsing, designing, etc.'

'There will be that.'

'I won't see you much.'

'There's that too.'

'I hope I don't have to book time to see you.' He tried to laugh.

'You won't,' I stated emphatically. 'That's why I said trial. If it gets too much, I cancel.'

'Okay.'

The following weekend, I sat down, planned, and plotted what life would be like until Christmas and it wasn't pretty. I showed Alex.

'Ouch!' he grimaced.

* * * * *

I performed at RPs twice more in September, to rave reviews and enthusiastic crowds. The RPs shows continued every fortnight until the end of the year. I debuted Prissy at the Buckingham on the first Friday in October (brought forward from the second) and was a hit from the first night. I then did shows at the Buckingham every fortnight, also until the end of the year. The following Thursday, Prissy debuted at the Governor Hotel. Whilst the reception was more subdued, being a slightly mellower mixed crowd, I agreed to do a fortnightly show at the Gov. I was happy with all the fortnightly arrangements as it gave me more time with Alex.

That changed by the end of September.

9. Troupe-ing the Wig.

By the end of September, I'd had a number of inquiries, from other drag queens, to join Prissy on stage. In addition, I'd only performed twice more since the debut. Was there some sort of grapevine out there that I didn't know of? I mean, I knew how the gay grapevine worked. It was the fastest in town. You want something out by word-of-mouth, tell a gay man! Oh, and make sure to tell him it's a secret. That will ensure even greater rapidity. I guess with a crowd as big as RPs gets, it was probably all over town by two a.m. anyway. No need to wait until Monday to start spreadin' the news.

Whatever happened, it was just as well I arrived early on the other two nights I was performing. RPs was quite full for nine-thirty. It astounded me the first time. Although I had said to Al that I wouldn't arrive in drag to a venue, I deliberately wanted to see what would happen if I did. Therefore, for the last performance in September, I rocked up at my usual time of nine-thirty, except this time in full costume.

Well, the reception was amazing. It must've taken me a good thirty minutes to get from the front door to the stairs. I was stopped for photos, kisses, hugs, you name it, and they wanted it. At one stage when I called for a path to be made, it appeared. I had never experienced anything like it before. Right then, I made the decision, that if I ever had my own club, there would be a stage door, for those that wanted to use it. I also decided that I would arrive a little earlier and dress on site, as I planned originally.

It's possible you may be wondering where this idea of owning my own club came from? Well, it was something that had been tossing around at the back of my mind since I debuted at RPs at the beginning of September. At university, I became involved with a theatre group on campus. Twice a year for the four years I was there, we ran a cabaret night. We ran it as a business. It got a number of students from different departments involved. Accounting, theatre, marketing, hospitality, you get the idea. It ran for three nights each week over two weeks. We only ever made a small profit, but we didn't mind. It was all about the experience. For me, it always stayed with me and suddenly resurfaced soon after my debut at RPs. So, the thing was at that point, how would it happen, if it was to happen?

Right, back to the requests to join Prissy on stage. There were seven actually. I'm not sure if I was surprised or offended.

'You look bewildered, hon, what is it?' asked Alex at lunch the day after my last show in September.

'I'm not sure how I'm feeling at the moment.'

'Do tell?'

'I know I should be flattered that I have these requests, then there's a part of me that's miffed that I don't have more.'

Alex laughed.

'It's not funny!'

'Yes it is sweetie.'

'What am I going to do, Alex?'

'What do you mean?'

'I have three successful shows running. The Gov and RPs Thursday and Saturday, respectively, followed by the Buckingham on the alternate Friday.'

'The bank balance is looking healthy.'

'True,' I agreed. 'Then I had to decline Devon's invitation

to work every Friday night. Now I have no less than seven requests, count them seven, from people who want to join me.'

'Do you want a troupe?' asked Alex.

'I don't know,' I said. 'I haven't thought about it.'

'If I may?'

I waved my hand for him to continue.

'RPs is covered as you are one of a group of performers,' he began.

I nodded.

'The Buckingham and The Gov it's only you. Looking at it from the outside, I'd say a troupe would be a good idea. For those shows, you've got others to perform with and if they become good enough, even perform on their own.'

I looked at Alex for quite some time, silent, staring at a point beyond his shoulder.

'What's wrong? Is there a bug on my nose? A witch on my shoulder? What?' He began checking his nose with crossed eyes and made sweeping motions across his shoulders.

I laughed. 'Nothing like that at all. I was thinking about what you said. Ever the practical one. I'll do it.'

'You will?'

'Yes.'

'Seven to choose from?' said Alex.

'I know. How the hell are we going to do that?' I let out a deep breath.

After lunch, we looked at the schedule for the rest of October.

'From what they've said in their initial emails, three are already performing. The other four have only been on stage for heats of the Miss Melvegas Drag contest, which they didn't win and which I didn't get to see.'

'How could you see them perform? You didn't know they were interested. We'll just have to let that one slide.'

I nodded. 'I've got email addresses for each of those interested. I'll ask them to send me some sort of resume.'

'That's a good start,' replied Alex.

'For the three already performing, we'll find out where they'll be and see them.'

'Agreed. And the other four?'

'We'll have to wait and see,' I replied.

'Hey, what about the fees?' Alex asked. 'Won't they change if you have a troupe?'

'What fees?'

'The fees you're being paid for working at the Buckingham and the Governor.'

'Hmmm, I should check.'

'It'd be advisable.'

'I'll suggest an adjusted fee scale and see how that goes.'

'That sounds like it should work.'

I sent the emails that Sunday afternoon. Within forty-eight hours, I had responses from all seven. 'The three current performers are all at different venues,' I relayed to Alex at dinner. 'The shows are all an hour apart. One performer is involved in an early show and the other two are later. They're also performing twice in October and on the same nights, the 6th and the 20th.'

'That's fortunate,' replied Alex.

'Very much so,' I said. 'By a stroke of fortune, the other four budding drag queens have been recalled for a second chance performance in the Miss Melvegas Drag contest. They're performing on October 12 and 18. This is going to work well, hon.'

'It sounds like it. Are you sure you want rookies?'

'I'm still a rookie.'

'I wouldn't say that.'

'I would,' I replied. 'They'll be a challenge.'

'There is that. Are you going to want help in deciding?'

'As if I'd leave you out of it? It'd be appreciated.'

'I think I can help.' Alex smiled. 'How are we going to

judge them?'

'I was thinking of drawing up a list of criteria and then marking each one on a scale of one to five.'

'Hmmmm.'

'Too complicated?'

'Depends on how long the list is.'

'I'll work on some ideas.'

'Sweet,' said Alex. 'By the way, have you heard back about the fees yet?'

'Yeah,' I replied. 'I got some emails today. Thankfully they're okay but they reserve the right to adjust who performs depending on crowds.'

'That's fair.'

'I don't have a problem with that either.'

* * * * *

By the end of October, I'd held 'healthy' conversations with Alex. 'Why are you being so pigheaded tonight?' I blurted out in frustration after another hour of heated debate.

'I'm deliberately playing devil's advocate for you,' he replied. 'I want you to be sure of who you're choosing. I could easily agree with many of your arguments and choices but you have to perform with them. You'll have to work with them day in day out.'

I stared at Alex. *Whoosh. All the air gone from my sails. How dare he be so practical!* 'I'm going for a walk,' I announced. I picked up my keys and phone and left the house.

'Welcome home, sweetie,' said Alex, appearing from the dining room when he heard me enter. 'This way,' he added, taking me by the hand.

I looked bewildered. 'I need to have a shower and cool down first.'

'Not yet,' he said calmly. He led me to the dining table

where seven photos lay. 'Choose.'

I looked at him dumbly.

'You haven't spent the last hour walking for the sake of walking,' he said. 'You were walking for the last hour to choose your back up troupe. So choose.'

I stared at the seven pictures on the table. 'This one, this one and this one.'

'Excellent. My choices as well. Now you can go and have that shower and we'll celebrate when you smell better.' Alex waved his hand under his nose.

'Bite me.' I slapped my hand on my rump as I went upstairs.

* * * * *

Shelby Wright was the first one I chose. Mick Sharpe, 32, stands at 185cm with an athletic build. In some respects, his drag name summed up the fact that he entered the Miss Melvegas Drag competition for fun. He didn't win his initial heat, or the second chance, nevertheless I could see that he could dance well and had a good stage presence. Whilst not having heard Mick sing, his resume indicated he'd performed in musical theatre when he was in high school and college.

Tanya Hide's was the second photo I slid across the table and out of the line-up. Rory Winston was the youngest we hired, at 21. Although much shorter than Mick, his 175cm frame was stocky and muscular. As his drag name suggests, I would've done that to him had he not have performed as well as he did. He sang live in his second chance and did a fantastic job. He didn't move that much whilst he performed, though I wasn't worried. His resume indicated a primary and early high school dance history.

Sam Booka was the last of my choices. Dean Jacobson 29 was another tall performer. He stood at 183cm and had a lean build. He was the only drag queen I chose that was currently performing. He moved well and gracefully. He kept in time with the other performers and handled himself well when alone. His mime was almost perfect. He told me he could sing, although preferred to mime. I liked his enthusiasm for the job.

10. Peter, Pastels and Performance Anxiety

In preparation for the staff function, I'd chosen to use the same design of costume for the girls as I had for Prissy's debut. The only difference was the colour. I had the bolder, brighter blue, and I wanted pastels for the girls. With the fact that I had only just sent the invitations to those I'd chosen, we hadn't even had a rehearsal yet. To say it was tense the day I spoke to Terese over the phone about them was an understatement.

'Let me see the guys first, then I can advise on the best colour for them,' she said calmly, after I'd explained what I wanted.

'As long as it's pastel, I'll be happy,' I replied, sternly

'We'll see.'

'No ... we ... won't.' I sat back in the chair and rapidly drummed the fingers of my free hand on my desk.

Terese responded graciously. 'I know what you want, sweetie, but let me tell you, pastels do not always work on everyone. If pastels look fine, then that's what we'll do. However...'

'There'll be no however, it's pastels.'

'When did you want to do this?' Terese had definitely moved on.

'I was hoping for next week?'

'Can I come to a rehearsal with samples?'

‘Of the pastels, sure. We start rehearsing from this coming Monday and continue on Wednesday this week. We’ll then probably practice each Monday and Wednesday from there on.’

‘Okay. I’ll give you a call to arrange the time.’

‘Bye.’ I disconnected my mobile and flung the wireless earpiece across the room. ‘Bloody fussy costume designers. Why the hell did I ever decide to do this.’

Alex came into the office, having heard the commotion. ‘What’s the matter?’

‘Your stupid sister, that’s what!’ I rose and stormed past him. ‘I’m going for a walk.’

Before Alex could say anything, I was gone. I came back a couple of hours later, just as hot and bothered as when I left – but for opposite reasons to why I’d left.

‘You didn’t take your phone with you?’ greeted Alex.

‘Why would I want to take that?’ I protested. ‘I wasn’t in the mood for talking to anyone.’

‘So I found out.’

‘Wha’d’ya mean?’ I challenged, when I came down from the shower.

‘Terese called after you left and she told me about your chat.’

‘I see. I ‘spose you’re on her side?’

‘Don’t start with me, sunshine. You’re the one being the diva all of a sudden.’

‘I am not a bleedin’ diva.’

‘Calm down, sweetie. I’m on your side.’

‘Good’

‘As much as hers.’

‘That’d be right.’

‘Terese can be just as pig-headed as you. Why won’t you listen to her?’

‘Why won’t she listen to me?

‘She was listening. You want all pastels for the troupe for their debut.’

'What's wrong with that?'

'Nothing's wrong with that, except you have to be open to the fact that pastels don't always work on everyone.'

'See, you are on her side.'

'I am not, hon. Pastels might work well with Rory's skin but put pastels on Mick and he'll wash out.'

'That's what make-up's for.'

'Not that much make-up.'

'We'll find out I'm right this week.'

'Yes dear.'

'Don't you "yes dear" me, Alex.'

Alex shrugged his shoulders. 'It's time for dinner, let's eat.'

* * * * *

'It's the last time we'll meet before next month's function,' began Sally, at the final committee meeting we held in early November. 'What have we got?' she asked.

'The venue is confirmed and paid for,' said Nick.

'The caterer is confirmed and a menu has been decided,' added Carmen, handing out menus to the committee.

'Looks good, Carmen,' said Sally. 'Peter, what have you got to report?'

'I have good news for you,' I replied.

'You have a drag queen?' asked Sally.

'I do.'

'Any details?'

'Yes.'

Sally, Carmen and Nick sat and stared at me. I smiled, knowing I was teasing them.

'And?'

'And what?'

'Do you have a name or what?'

'Yes I do.'

Sally looked at me, her hands open in a gesture of

impatient inquiry. 'And?'

'Oh, you want the name, do you?'

'YES!' they said in unison.

I laughed. 'Her name is Prissy DuPonce. She's new on the circuit and I've just recently found out that she now has a troupe backing her.'

'That's a bit dangerous, isn't it?'

'She's very popular and quite good,' I responded.

'Have you seen her perform?' asked Nick.

'Sort of.'

'Sort of? What does that mean?'

'I haven't seen her perform personally. I was at a crowded venue where I heard her, I just couldn't see her.'

'She was good?' asked Sally.

'The crowd certainly thought so.'

'It should be a good afternoon then.'

'I think so,' I agreed. 'I just need to pass on the details to her management. Do you know if we can get access early? In case she needs to prepare?'

'Yeah,' said Nick, sliding a piece of paper to me. 'I thought this information might be needed.'

'Thanks. I'll pass it on. Prissy has asked for only one thing.'

'What's that, Peter?' asked Sally.

'That her arrival be kept a surprise. She thinks it'll work better if no one knows she's going to be there.'

'I guess we can do that? It might add to the afternoon.'

'Good, I'll let her know.'

* * * * *

I'd negotiated with Devon, owner of the Buckingham Hotel, to use a disused function room on the first floor as a rehearsal room. Before our first rehearsal, I'd spent a few nights rearranging the room so that we all had a table and a clothes rack. The first meeting was a get to know you night. Listening to the music I wanted, the style of shows I wanted. I listened to their thoughts and concerns as well.

Walking around the room this particular night, having had the venue details confirmed that day, I pondered all that was before me. Before us. It was then I noticed a parcel just inside the door I hadn't seen on entry. I picked it up and placed it on a table. Upon opening it, I began to laugh.

'What's so funny?' asked Dean, as he, and the others, entered the room.

'This is?' I stood back and indicated the box on the table. 'I asked for a dozen sets. I didn't think the salesperson over the phone understood me properly.'

'What did they send?' queried Mick.

'A dozen boxes,' I replied. 'A dozen boxes, of a dozen sets of false eyelashes.'

'It seems they've thrown in a dozen applicators as well,' added Dean, looking further into the box.

'What are we going to do with so many sets of false eyelashes?' asked Rory.

I turned to face him, a hand on my tilted hip, an eyebrow raised and the smirk of having heard the most ridiculous thing.

Rory looked a little mortified, Dean rather sniggered and Mick was about to laugh.

Rory suddenly realised what he'd said. 'Oh yeah, I guess we will use them.'

I smiled, clapped him lightly on the shoulder and moved away from the table. 'Get you gear sorted and let's get started.'

The boys put their bags down and started to get ready.

'By the way, it's all go, guys.'

'Why, what's happened?' asked Dean.

'Nothing serious. The final details for the function were confirmed at a committee meeting at work today.'

'Ah.'

'Mick and Dean, I'd like you to make contact with the venue. Here are the details. Make sure we have all we need.'

'As in?' asked Mick.

'Change rooms, early access, entry and exit points to the stage. Things like that.'

Mick looked at Dean. 'We can do that.'

'Great. Let me know when you're done.'

* * * * *

I'm going to make this bit quick. I was wrong. Terese came to the first Monday night rehearsal we had and ... well ... I was wrong. Even the troupe seemed against me ... on the very first night too. It would seem that everyone else was right and I was wrong. I wasn't going to be able to have the girls in pastels as I wanted. Pastels looked great on Rory. Either pastels or bold suited Dean. Funnily enough, pastels did wash out Mick. Needless to say, I was wrong.

'I'm going to say this only once,' I announced as I walked in the door that night. 'I was wrong.'

Alex chuckled.

'It's not funny.'

'It is, sweetie. You were so adamant the other night that nothing was going to change your mind.'

'When you're conspired against by everyone, what choice does one have?'

'No one was conspiring against you, sweetie. You just didn't want to listen to reason. Perhaps now you'll listen to Terese. Isn't that why you decided to let her make your clothes? She does know what she's doing.'

'Perhaps.'

Alex smiled and shook his head.

* * * * *

At rehearsal the following Monday night, Mick and Dean reported their findings.

'We got a look at the stage and how big it was. I took some measurements and drew a line on the floor.'

'Let's see,' I said, looking at the line Mick had drawn. 'It's a smaller area than what we're used too but I think we can manage,' I said. 'Anything else?'

'The changing rooms they have will be large enough and will allow us to enter from the rear of the audience.'

'That's very good. I want to make a grand entrance and really give them something to talk about.'

The troupe laughed with me.

'We can also arrive up to an hour before the function starts to set up.'

'That's important, I want to make sure no one sees us, particularly me, arrive.'

* * * * *

The following night, Alex and I were at the Buckingham for their Tuesday Trivia Night with Chrissy and Billie, and Mick and Aidan, Mick's boyfriend.

'Let's hope this one isn't as eventful as the last time we were here,' I remarked.

'Why, what happened?' queried Mick.

'The last time were here for a trivia night, Devon wanted to know about the new drag queen he'd seen at RPs the previous Saturday night,' I explained.

'When was this? What new drag queen?' said Aidan.

I let my shoulders sink in resignation and looked at Aidan from under my eyebrows. 'Who do you think it might've been?'

'Ohh, you,' he replied, smiling.

'Anyhoo, we swore him to secrecy when he told us he wanted Prissy for here.'

'As you would,' chimed in Chrissy.

'Here he comes now, perhaps we'll all be privy to the next exciting instalment,' said Billie.

I turned to see Devon sauntering his way to our table in the back corner.

'In the corner again I see,' Devon greeted.

'Hello to you too,' I said.

'I hope you have a good night.'

'So do we. I could do with a meat tray and a bar tab.'

The group laughed.

'Hey, Pete, have you got a moment?' asked Devon.

'Sure.' I got up and followed him to a quieter corner. 'What's up?'

'How are things looking for Christmas?'

'Well, we can do all the Fridays, the Sunday before Christmas, Christmas eve, but not Christmas night.'

'New Year's eve?'

'Yeah, that's cool.'

'Great. Somethin' else I want you and Alex ta know before anyone.'

'Should I go and get Alex?'

'Nah. Thing is, I'm thinking of giving up the Buckingham and selling her.'

'You're selling her? Who to?'

'I was kind of hopin' you two might be interested?'

'Me? Us?' I sputtered.

'Go home, talk about it and let me know. '

'Um ... err... okay.' I was startled.

11. Pubs and Prangs

'Like I said, go home and talk about it. There's no rush to answer tomorrow, or anythin' like that,' added Devon.

'We will.' I was still a bit stunned.

'I'd better get on and make sure all my guests are happy.'

I watched as Devon mingled, chatting to tables dotted about the room. I returned to the table. Mick had disappeared and soon returned with a tray of drinks, just as Devon stepped onto the stage to begin the games.

Alex noted I was looking a little stunned. 'What's the matter?'

I leant in, indicating for the others to do so as well. 'I've just been given the most startling offer. Devon wants to sell the pub and he wants Alex and I to have first option.'

The gasps were audible and I began to flap about for quiet.

'A toast to the new owners of the Buckingham,' Mick said quietly.

'We're not there yet,' stated Alex.

'You will be though,' insisted Mick. 'You'd be great at it.'

Everyone else cheered, drawing looks from other tables nearby.

'Save the celebrations until *after* we've decided what to do,' I said

We left Devon with his offer ringing in our ears. I had no idea what Alex was thinking but I couldn't stop. *Why does he want us to have it? What are we going to do with a pub?* We were both silent in the car on the way home.

'Well, what do you think?' asked Alex, as we walked inside.

'I really don't know,' I replied.

'Why don't we sleep on it and see how we feel in the morning.'

'Good idea, hon.'

We went upstairs but I couldn't sleep that well. For the record, neither did Alex.

I stumbled into the kitchen, still trying to make sense of the day.

'Extra strong, double sugar,' said Alex, handing me some coffee.

I took a sip and began to feel better.

'You couldn't sleep much either?' he queried.

'You noticed, huh?'

'Just a tad. I was almost going to go and sleep in the spare bed.'

'One more kick in the back and I was about to throw you out.'

We smiled at each other.

'Well then, what are we going to do about it?'

'What, the sleeping problems?'

'Not exactly, however certainly the problem that caused the sleeping problem.'

'Oh, that problem. Well, I'll give Devon a call and see what he wants for the place,' I said.

'I'll give the lawyers a call and see when we can talk to them about it.'

'Hopefully we'll have Devon's price before then.'

'I'll also get a valuer in to check it out for us.'

It took me from the Wednesday morning at breakfast until almost midday Friday to get Devon on the phone.

'You're a hard man to track down, Devon,' I said when I finally managed to speak with him.

'Sorry about that, Pete, I've been busy with a few family things,' he replied.

'All good I hope?'

'Nothing serious.'

'Good.'

'What did you want to know? Have you thought more about my question the other day?'

'About selling us the Buckingham?'

'Yeah, that one.'

'We have actually.'

'And?'

'We happen to be interested.'

'That's great news.'

'I have two requests.'

'Yes?'

'How much do you want? And, we'd like to have an independent valuation.'

'I have no problems with the second request.'

'Cool.'

'As to the first, $1.7m.'

I baulked as I went to take a drink.

'Too much?' asked Devon.

'Not at all. I was expecting more.'

'I'm sure it's worth more, however I'd really like to know it's going to a couple of good blokes. Not to mention a fantastic drag queen.'

'Thanks.'

'Prissy has really brought in lots more people, particularly on a Friday night.'

'So why sell?'

'It's time.'

'I can appreciate that. When do you want a decision from us?'

'When you're ready. I'm not in a hurry to sell.'

'I'll let you know once I've had a good chat with Alex.'

'Let me know and dinner, or lunch, will be on me at The Corset and Tassel?'

'I think we can deal with that. I'll make arrangements for a valuer to get in contact with you soon.'

'Very good.'

'I got on to Devon today,' I announced when Alex got home from work.

'Great. What did he say?'

'Devon wants to offer it to us for $1.7m.'

'What?'

'Too much? That's what Devon thought.'

'No, too little.'

'That's what I said. He wants to make sure it goes to good hands. I think if he was to put it on the open market, he'd ask for much more.'

'When is the valuation?'

'Don't know yet. I'll make some calls on Monday. Hopefully we can get it sorted out quickly.'

'Speaking of Monday, we have an appointment with the lawyers at five. Can you make that?'

'I'll make sure I do.'

* * * * *

I arrived at the lawyers just before five and went in to see if Alex had arrived. He hadn't, so I let the receptionist know I was there and sat down.

Just after five, our lawyer came to the waiting room. 'Hi, Peter, it's good to see you again.'

'It's good to see you too Beverley. Alex isn't here yet

though.'

'That's okay, we'll give him another five minutes or so. I still have a few things to finish from today, I'll do those and come back out.'

'Sounds good.'

I sat down and sent Alex an SMS to see how long he'd be. After five minutes, when Beverley returned, he still hadn't arrived.

"I'm not sure what's keeping him tonight. Rather than waste time, we'll give you a call to reschedule.'

'We can wait another five or ten,' she offered.

'Uhm, no, I don't want to keep you hanging around just for the sake of it.'

'I have things I can do.'

'We'll reschedule, that way you can leave when you want to.'

'If you're sure?'

'I am.'

'He could be stuck in traffic.'

'He would've been here by now or let me know he was running late. We'll call you back.

I sent Alex another SMS as I left the lawyers and got on a tram for home. I wasn't concerned that I didn't hear from him immediately. When he gets busy, he doesn't see or hear his mobile. There was no Alex when I got home either. *Never mind. I'll start dinner anyway.* I went upstairs and had a shower. When I came into the kitchen, Alex still wasn't home. I sat and watched the news, checking dinner now and then.

Just as the weather came on, I picked up the phone to answer it. 'Yes, this is Peter Long-Smith.'

'It's Mary from the Albert Hospital.'

'The Albert Hospital, what's happened?' I replied, beginning to panic. 'Who's injured?'

'I need to confirm some details first.'

'Um ... okay.'

'Are you related to Alex Long-Smith?'

'Yes, he's my partner. What's happened to him?'

'He's been involved in an accident.

'Is he okay?'

'He's resting now.'

'Am I able to come and visit him?'

'You can, however be aware that he may have some amnesia.'

'As a result of the accident?'

'He received a mild concussion and sometimes amnesia can result, especially after this type of accident.'

'Is he all right?'

'Yes, it will probably only be his immediate short term memory that will be affected.'

'Does he still know who I am?'

'Yes, that's how we got your information.'

'I understand.'

'When you arrive, go to the front desk and they will direct you.'

'Thank you.' I replaced the handset and began to run in a hundred directions at once.

Amidst my confusion, the phone rang again. 'Hello,' I said, sounding rushed.

'Have you stopped running around yet?' said the voice.

'What? Who?'

'You heard me.'

'Who is this?' I asked.

'That's rich.'

'Huh?'

'You don't even know your own partner's voice over the phone. I'm crushed.'

'Alex, I'm sorry dear.'

'Sit down.'

'I am.'

'No you're not. Sit!'

I sat down. 'How did you know?'

'Sweetie? Now that I have you sitting down, I also know you've stopped running around.'

'Are you okay?'

'My head's a little sore and things are fuzzy.'

'At least you remember who I am.'

'I could never forget you. Now, have you turned the dinner off yet?'

'Yes. I managed to do that in the first few moments after I got the call.'

'Good.'

'As soon as I get off the phone to you, I'm coming to the hospital. What room are you in?'

'Three North, room seventeen, bed by the window.'

'Okay, see you soon.'

'Take your time. I love you.'

'I'll be careful. Love you too.'

Yes, dinner is turned off. Message bank is on. Keys. Wallet. Phone. I think I can go now.

Murphy had it in for me that night, I'm sure of it. I seemed to catch every red light from home to the hospital. Then to add insult to injury, every driver ahead of me was going far slower than I wanted. One thing going in my favour was that the car park attached to the hospital was open 24 hours.

I walked, well almost ran, to the main desk and confirmed Alex's room. The I went to the nurse's station. After confirming the location of the room, I walked past the empty bed and saw Alex relaxing. When he saw me, he smiled broader than I had ever seen.

'Hon, I'm glad you're okay.' I said.

'I'm glad you're here.'

We hugged tightly and shed a tear.

'What's the goss then?' I asked, sitting on the bed.

'All I've been told is that I was in a car accident this afternoon.'

'Who with?'

'I don't remember' said Alex.

'Do you know where you were going?'

'Nope. Do you know where I was going?'

'I suppose you were leaving work, as you were to meet me at the lawyers.'

'Why would we want to meet with the lawyers?'

'Don't you remember the conversation with Devon the other night?' I said.

'When did we see Devon?'

'On Tuesday at the Buckingham's trivia night. Chrissy, Billie, Mick and Aidan were all there.'

'Were they? How are they?'

'Fine.'

'We must catch up with them soon,' continued Alex.

'We'll come back to that conversation later,' I said. 'Well, the reason we were meeting the lawyers was because we were going to discuss the option of buying the Buckingham from Devon.'

'When did Devon put it up for sale?'

'He hasn't yet, he's offered it to us first.'

'When did he do that?'

'At the trivia night ... never mind. He's offered it to us first. Perhaps we should talk about this when you're better.'

'Why would we want to buy a hotel?'

'Don't worry your pretty little head about it.'

'You think I'm pretty then?'

'Of course I do, sweetie.'

'That's nice.'

'How long are you going to be in hospital?'

'I think the doctor said about a week.'

* * * * *

'Ugh.' I flopped heavily onto the chair beside Alex's

hospital bed. It was the Wednesday after the accident. I'd been at rehearsals, but had called it early. Alex's amnesia was rapidly abating, which was good to know. The nurses had said he was recovering very well indeed.

'I wasn't expecting to see you tonight,' said Alex, turning towards me. 'What happened?'

'I called an early finish to rehearsal and we're not meeting again until next Monday night. We're all tired and busy.'

'I'd go and make you a cuppa but it's a tad difficult at the moment.' Alex indicated his position in bed.

I relaxed a little and laughed. 'I couldn't move if I tried.'

'Now, what's the matter?'

'Too much rehearsal.'

'Too much? How can that be? You've only had … what is it … five, including tonight's? How can five be too much?

'I don't know.'

'Are you being a dragon again?'

'Excuse me,' I said sitting up. 'I am not a dragon!'

'Sweetie, I've seen you in similar situations, you can be a dragon. You want the end result from the first day.'

'No I don't, do I?' I relaxed back into the chair

'Sometimes you do and I suspect this is one of those occasions. What are the boys doing then?'

'They're trying hard.'

'Have you got any video of the rehearsals yet?'

'Yeah, I took some tonight.' I reached over the side of the chair and grabbed my bag. From it, I pull out the video recorder.

'Let's have a look then,' said Alex.

I pressed the play button and for about ten minutes or so, we watched part of that evening's rehearsals.

'I've seen enough.'

I pressed stop. 'What have you seen enough of?' I dared to ask.

'Well, you're not being as much of a dragon as I thought.'

'Ha!' I said triumphantly.

'But at the same time you are.'

I turned to him, extremely puzzled. 'Are you sure you haven't taken more drugs than you're supposed to? Do I need to get a nurse to check that bruise on your noggin? The concussion seems to have affected your ability to make sense.'

'You're so funny sometimes, it hurts.'

'Eh, bite me.'

'Later. From what I saw, you were giving fair and detailed instructions. Sometimes over and over, although understandable. What I think you've inadvertently done is placed an expectation on the guys that they need to get this right and get it right quickly.'

'I don't think I said it that way exactly.'

'You may not have but that's what comes across.'

'How can you tell?'

'The boys are concentrating too hard on the steps and the music. They need to learn to relax more. When are they being debuted?'

'At the staff function.'

'Hmmm.'

'What?'

'Perhaps you should debut them earlier, make sure they can actually perform in front of a crowd. You want them to be the best possible for the function, right?'

'Yeah. Anything less and I'd have egg on my face. Maybe you're right. Maybe I do need to get them on stage before the function.'

'Try them at RPs or the Buckingham in the weeks leading up to the work do.'

'Perhaps. I don't want to think about that right now.'

'Fair enough.'

'I'm going home to have a hot bath and go to bed.'

'Good idea.'

I kissed him goodnight and headed home.

*****

The following day I called Karl.

'This is a person-to-person call for Ms Peachy Keen,' I said into the phone whilst holding my nose.

'From whom is the call?' inquired Karl.

'Madame Prissy DuPonce,' I continued nasally.

'Please connect her.'

'One moment. Click,' I said mockingly and then added, 'Bing bong, bing bong, bing bong, bing bong.' I could hear Karl chuckling. 'Connecting you now.'

'Thank you.'

'Peachy, is that you my dear?'

'Prissy hon, how's it swinging?'

'It's not.'

'I'm sorry to hear that.'

'It's life in a body glove.'

Karl laughed hard. I joined him.

'One day ....'

'...I'm gonna get caught with my skirt down. Yeah I know.'

'How are you doing, Peter?'

'Really well thanks, Karl.'

'How's Alex? I heard he was in an accident last week.'

'He's much better thanks. He's getting back to his old self.'

'He been giving you cheek then?'

'When doesn't he.'

'I'm happy to hear he's doing well.'

'Thanks. Can I ask you something?'

'Last time you said something like that, I had to make room on my stage for some tart.'

'Pffft.'

'What is it?'

'I was wondering if Peachy would be willing to allow Prissy to show her troupe at RPs?'

'How long is the show?' asked Karl.

'About thirty minutes.'
'Could you do both shows?'
'Sure.'
'Great. I'll intro and do the ads and shit, then it's all yours.'
'Hopefully it'll be accepted.'
'I don't think that'll be a problem. You're quite a hit.'
'Thanks. I'm blushing now.'
Karl laughed, 'When did you want to show the troupe?'
'I was hoping for the first Saturday in December.'
'I can deal with that.'
'That's great. The guys will be happy.'
'Done.'

12. Yeth Mathter

'Hi honey I'm homo,' I called as I walked in the door after work on Monday, having brought Alex home from the hospital the day before.

'Good, I need my jug of water refilled.'

'Yes, I'm well thanks. I had a good day at work. How was your day?'

'Sorry dear, it's been kinda lonely here.'

'Well not anymore.'

'Why's that?' asked Alex.

'I managed to get a week's leave.'

'You didn't have to do that.' Alex sounded slightly annoyed.

'Yes I did.'

'No you didn't.'

'It's done now and I'm not changing it.'

'It will be nice to have you around.'

'Yes it will. How've you been feeling today?

'Apart from bored and lonely?'

'Apart from bored and lonely.'

'Better than I thought actually,' explained Alex.

'No headaches?'

'Not really. Only when I get up too fast. I just had to take it slowly when I moved.'

'I'll get you going.'

'Thanks, I think.'

I laughed. 'What do you want for dinner?'

'I managed to take some steak out earlier.'

'Steak and vegies it is. Although I do have rehearsal tonight.'

'Then you'd better get on with it.'

'Yeth, mathter,' I mocked and bowed before him.

'Did you call a valuer today?'

'No, I had to make sure that things were done before I went on leave. We can do that tomorrow.'

'I was thinking it might be good to reschedule that appointment with our lawyer and go and see the accountant about the Buckingham.'

'Good idea, sweetie. Glad I thought of it.'

'Whatever.'

I chuckled.

*****

'Thank you,' I said, as we took a break during the rehearsal that night. 'I'm sorry I lost my cool last week. I can be a bit of a perfectionist sometimes.'

'I think we all needed the break,' replied Mick.

'I'm happy it's coming together so well though,' I said. 'I showed some of the video of last Wednesday's rehearsal to Alex and he picked up on a couple of things.'

'What were they?' asked Dean.

'He said that I must've implied a high level of response from you guys without actually asking for it.'

'Oh?' asked Mick.

'Yeah,' I replied. 'He noticed that all of you were concentrating harder than usual on getting everything right.'

'Well we do want to get everything right,' added Mick.

'I have no doubt about that Mick, although you don't have to put yourselves into an early grave to do it.' I smiled. Thankfully, they all smiled with me. 'Of course I want everything to be just right, nevertheless I also want you guys to enjoy what you do. I've seen you all on stage and I chose you three because of what I saw.'

'Thanks, Peter,' said Rory.

'Let's work hard, and enjoy it at the same time,' I encouraged. 'I have something else I'd like to discuss with you guys.'

They gathered chairs and we sat around the table. 'I want to debut you guys on the last Friday in November at the Buckingham and the following Saturday at RPs.'

'Really?'

'That's great.'

'Are we ready?'

'By then, I'm sure we'll be ready.' I was enthusiastic. 'Besides, I think we need to perform before my work function.'

'Will we do the show anywhere else?'

'Let's see how the Buckingham and RPs go first.'

'We'd need to work on more material, won't we?' asked Rory.

'If this works, I doubt we'd be allowed to just disappear again, only to come out on special occasions. We'd probably need to introduce a new routine every 6-8 weeks,' I explained.

'That's a lot of work,' responded Dean.

'More than likely,' I said. 'If this is a success, are you still committed to working with me?'

'Yes.' Mick, Dean and Rory responded in unison.

That's good to hear,' I said. 'I've spoken with Peachy and she's happy for us to take over for a night, hence the fairly specific dates.'

'What would you have done if we said no?' asked Dean.

'I would've thought of something else.'

'I guess we should rehearse then,' added Mick.

'We could fall flat on our collective arses,' I suggested.

'Then let's make sure we don't,' encouraged Rory. 'Once

more tonight?'

We rehearsed for another hour or so. This time, we pretended we were performing for someone and that they were responding to our performance. I encouraged the troupe to imagine the reflection of themselves in the mirrors was the audience. This seemed to allow them to lift a gear. The air was filled with excitement after the first run through. We discussed a few points, made a couple of changes and did it again. When we finished, I could tell everyone was enthusiastic.

* * * * *

We came home from the lawyers feeling thrilled.

'I'm glad they think it'd be a good idea,' said Alex.

'It'll be an interesting chapter of life if we go ahead.'

'Why shouldn't we?'

'Just being cautious.'

Alex smiled. 'What about contacting a valuer?'

'We can try the one the lawyers gave us?'

'It's a start. At least they thought it was a good idea.'

'Yeah. I'll give them a call after lunch.'

'Why don't you do it now, I'll get lunch ready. The sooner we make contact the sooner we'll have an answer.'

I went and rang the valuer we had the details for. Alex was just finishing placing sandwich stuff on the table when I returned.

'What did they say?'

'They'd be happy to do it for us.'

'That's great. When can they check it out?'

'Monday.'

'That soon.'

'I was quite surprised. Whilst I was on the phone, they checked and found that there had been a cancellation that morning and the valuer could have a look at the property Monday afternoon. I just have to send all the details to them by email.'

'Is it going to cost much?'

'Not really.'

13. Pheasant Plucking

The Poncettes were being debuted at the Buckingham at the end of November. We had routines prepared, I wanted the very first song the girls performed to be bold, spectacular and ridiculously funny. I found the perfect song and presented the idea to them only two weeks before the Buckingham show.

'We can't learn it that quickly?' said Mick.

'Of course you can,' I replied. 'I know it's a little on the ridiculous side, nevertheless I reckon that'll help in learning it.'

'Where did you get this?' queried Dean, a little startled and stifling a giggle.

I laughed. 'I heard it on JAY a while ago and trawled the net ...'

'... I always thought you were a trawler ...' laughed Mick.

'... yeah, yeah. Anyway, I trawled the net and eventually found the words and the song. It took me a little longer to get the music but I have it. I was going to do it on my own but I think you girls will do just fine.'

'There's four parts and only three of us?' indicated Rory.

'You're not totally on your own. I'll be there,' I encouraged. 'I'll do the first and last parts.'

'When are we doing this in the show?' asked Mick.

'I thought we could open with this one?'

'We could but what about costumes,' Mick added.

'Already thought of that too.' I smiled. 'We'll have the dresses for the rest of the routine on underneath a large, loose peasant-looking frock. When the number's finished, you race off, remove the frock and come back on stage. I can stay and chat for a moment and when I see you're ready, we can swap. We can rearrange the order of the songs easily enough so that the song following this new one will be the one where you three start to sing and I join later. That way, after I finish chatting, I leave the stage and change. I couldn't pass up the song.'

'It's good,' agreed Dean. 'Perhaps we can work it so we finish with the new song?'

'Hmmm,' I thought aloud. 'Yes, we can do that a little better. There's a piano intro. When I have the backing track arranged, I can extend the piano intro to give us time to finish changing and get the stage set up.'

'Yeah, that'll work,' said Mick, excited.

'Then you're happy to do this new song?'

'Yes,' they all agreed.

When we arrived at the Buckingham for the girl's debut performance, everyone was excited. We settled into the familiar surrounds of our dressing rooms upstairs.

'Time to go girls,' I announced. They all began to breathe deeply. 'Relax and enjoy yourselves. You know what crowds are like. Just do what you've rehearsed.'

I walked on stage to a rousing reception. 'Oh, you're too kind boys. A girl'll get a big head if you carry on that like.' I placed my hand over my crotch. The crowd wolf-whistled. 'I have a treat for you tonight. So that you don't get sick of looking at me all the time, I have some new faces for you to look at. Tonight you will witness the birth of the Poncettes.' The crowd cheered and hollered. 'Let's not keep you waiting. Welcome my girls, Tanya Hide, Shelby Wright and Sam Booka, the Poncettes ...' I stepped aside to allow the girls to flow onto the stage. I stood back and watched as they kissed and caroused their way past audience members closest to the stage.

I nodded to the sound man and we began. It was heartening to see the crowd bop and cheer with the girls and I, as we moved through our routine. They left the stage to a raucous reception.

'Wha'd'ya think of that? Huh?' The crowd whistled and cheered some more. I distinctly heard 'encore' above the din. 'Keep your panties on, they'll be back shortly with a very special number for you. Don't go away, we'll be right back.'

I left the stage and saw the girls ready for the next song. They raced past me to the stage as I furiously changed into my peasant costume. Just before I went back on stage, I sent the message for the music to start. I walked on and could see the confused, yet amused looks on everyone's faces as we got ready. Even I was chuckling a little bit. The music swelled and I began …

'Me 'usband is a farmer, he's a very busy man
I try to understand him and I help him all I can,
But sometimes in an evening I feel a trifle dim
All alone, I'm plucking pheasants, when I'd rather pluck with him.'

I could sense the crowd laughing as I held my skirt up and swayed back and forth, the pigtails attached to my wig swaying in time. The girls joined me …

'I'm not a pheasant plucker, I'm a pheasant plucker's mate
I'm only plucking pheasants 'cos the pheasant plucker's late!'

The girls then came forward, one by one, to present their verses. As they were singing, I was busily stuffing feathers up my skirt and trying to hold them there. Then I stepped forward to finish the song …

'My boyfriend's in the forest always banging with his gun
If he could hear me half the time, I'm sure that he would run,

For there's fluff in all my crannies, there's feathers up my nose
And I'm itching in the kitchen from my head down to my toes.

I'm not a pheasant plucker, I'm a pheasant plucker's wife
And when we pluck together, it's a pheasant plucking life!

I'm not a pheasant plucker, I'm a pheasant plucker's wife
And when we pluck together it's a pheasant plucking life!'

When the music stopped, the cheering was frantic. I could see that some people were laughing so hard, they were wiping tears from their eyes.

'You like that?'

'We want more pleasant ph ...'

'I'll have none of that language, thank you very much!' They laughed more. 'You might get some more pheasant plucking later.'

'Yes! More. We want pheasant plucking.'

'Give a big hand for the Poncettes, they'll be back again in the second show. We'll see you soon.'

The crowd cheered and we left the stage.

In the dressing room, we collapsed into our seats laughing.

'That went over better than I thought,' I said.

'It was so much fun,' agreed Mick. 'Maybe we can do a whole show based on bawdy bar songs?'

'You find them and I'll see what we can do,' I said. 'Let's get changed and be ready for the next show in thirty minutes. You can go and mingle and chat, but I want you back here in twenty minutes.'

The girls changed and went downstairs to their adoring fans. I changed more slowly, came downstairs, found Alex and had a drink with him and friends of ours.

The second show was as big a hit as the first. The girls were more relaxed and performed so much better. Yes, we did an encore performance of the pheasant song. We didn't bother changing costumes and it was rather fun doing it in showgirl costumes.

* * * * *

Ten days after calling the valuer to look at the Buckingham, we received his report. We had asked him to consider only the physical aspect of the Buckingham, as we already had a good idea of the value of the business.

'What's he say?' asked Alex excitedly, as I opened the letter.

'Give me a moment.' I began to read the details.

'It'll be on the last page.'

'I know that. Ah, here it is, $1m.'

'Hmm, I thought it would've been more than that.'

'Yeah, but what he says is fairly accurate.'

'Oh?'

'Nothing major. He's noted some of the stuff I'd already seen regarding the age of the building.'

'Fair enough.'

'Do you still want to accept $1.7m?' I said.

'Can we offer him $1.5m?'

'I think so.'

'Let's start at $1.4m and if he offers $1.5 or even $1.55m we accept. You okay with that?' suggested Alex.

'Very much so. We'd better get the lawyers on to it.'

'I'll call them.' Alex hobbled off to the office.

'What did they say?' I asked when he returned.

'They'll draw up a letter of offer for us to collect tomorrow afternoon.'

'Good. Then we can take it straight to Devon.'

* * * * *

'Thanks for meeting us so soon Devon.' I said as we greeted him at The Corset and Tassel for dinner.

'More than happy,' replied Devon. 'Do you have the results of the valuation?'

'We do,' said Alex.

'Good news?'

'We think so.'

'We want to make you an offer,' I added.

'That's good,' said Devon. 'What is it?'

'$1.4m,' I said.

'Hmm. What about $1.6m?'

'$1.5m?'

'$1.55m?' countered Devon.

I looked at Alex. 'Done.'

Devon stood. 'Done,' offering his hand. We shook. 'That was quick.'

'It was. Hope it wasn't too quick,' I replied.

'Not for me, mate,' added Devon. 'I prefer business to be quick. I hate drawn out affairs that take days to deal with offers and counter-offers. That's why I was really hoping you'd agree to buy the place.'

'Here we are. Five minutes into our meeting and the deal's done.'

'That only means we get to enjoy dinner without any hassles, or pervading thoughts of what is to come.'

'I'll drink to that,' said Alex, raising his glass. Devon and I followed.

'We've had our lawyers draw up an official letter of offer for you,' I informed.

'You've thought about this haven't you?'

'Like you didn't?'

Devon smiled.

'Guess it's up to the lawyers,' I said.

'I'm sure it'll work out fine,' said Devon.

* * * * *

We performed the two other routines the following week at RPs. I had the pheasant song just in case and the crowd there were almost begging us to perform it. So we did, at the end of the second routine. I'd say that many of our audience saw us at both venues, hence the fervour for which the pheasant song was requested.

I decided to keep the troupe exclusive to Friday's at the Buckingham. That way Peachy could have her stage back. The crowds swelled at the Buckingham when word got out that Prissy DuPonce and the Poncettes were performing there.

Alex and I had arrived at RPs at our normal time, about nine-thirty-ish. The guys arrived soon after. I moved through the thin crowd quickly, not really taking note of who was there. I went upstairs as normal and Alex came with me. Once I'd settled, Alex went back downstairs. Everything was as it usually was.

I was waiting downstairs with Peachy and the Poncettes.

'You ready for tonight, Prissy dear?' asked Peachy.

'Yeah,' I replied.

'That's good,' said Peachy. 'If you need any help, I can let you have a look at my CD collection.'

'I think I'll be fine.'

As I waited, I peered through the crowd and saw Alex. He turned to see me looking and smiled. I began to smile but froze mid-way through. I could see Alex looking at me oddly and he started to move towards me, but the music started, so he stopped. I stood transfixed, staring at a spot beyond his shoulder. Standing there were the committee and their partners.

I was surprised. As I continued to watch, I saw Nick tap Alex on the shoulder. He turned and acknowledged Nick. I found out after the show that Alex had told my work colleagues that I wasn't well and was resting at home. I heard the introduction and made my way down the hall to the stage. We performed the first routine and the Poncettes were accepted as equally as I was. It was a relief to see the crowd's reaction.

I was upstairs changing after the shows were finished when I sent Alex an SMS. 'Are they still there?'

'Yes,' replied Alex. 'They're having another drink. Will let you know when to come down.'

I sat back.

'What's the matter dear?' asked Peachy, seeing my concerned face.

'My friends from work were here tonight and they don't know who I am on stage. I can't go downstairs just yet.'

'I understand.' Peachy touched me on the shoulder and left the room.

Alex eventually came to the changing room and I was able to go home. The troupe had left as soon as the shows were finished. I called in sick for work Monday and Tuesday so I could concentrate on the function.

For the staff function, Aidan, who now knew the show, acted as our 'manager' and onsite contact. Aidan was also beginning to get involved administratively and his help with some of the office stuff was appreciated. I discovered he'd been involved in the Melvegas theatre industry and had some useful contacts. He liaised with my own contacts to ensure that we weren't breaching copyright with the music.

14. Daaarlings and Deceptions

Being an afternoon function, I'd invited the guys over for brunch before we left. We arrived at the venue an hour before anyone from work was due to show up, and were shown to our changing rooms and began to get ready. Aidan left to meet the committee and go over the program.

'I'm baaack,' said Aidan entering the room.

'How's it going downstairs?' I asked.

'The committee want to meet you.'

'We're finished in here, let them in.'

'Okay.'

'Wait. I noticed a lounge next door, we'll be in there.'

Aidan nodded and left. We finished dressing and moved to the lounge.

'Is it okay to come in?' called Aidan.

I opened the door and Aidan brought the committee in. Carmen, Sally and Nick were noticeably excited.

'Is this all the committee?' I asked.

'No,' replied Sally. 'Peter couldn't be here today. He's off sick at the moment.'

'I hope he gets well soon,' I acknowledged. 'It would've been nice to meet him.'

Sally handed me a piece of paper. 'I was wondering if you might use some of this info today?'

I looked at the paper and smiled. 'I think I can handle that dear,' I said.

We had arranged for Prissy and the Poncettes to enter from the rear and interrupt the proceedings. We were going to help them present their awards and recognitions. Aidan had left and gone downstairs and when he returned, we moved to the back of the room. We met Aidan, who made sure our radio mics were secured and switched on.

I took a deep breath and barged in. I flounced heavily down the aisle, air-kissing people as I went and flirting heavily. 'Daaarlings,' I cried.

Everyone turned to see this dark suited woman in heels and high wig making her way down the aisle.

'It's so good to see you all this afternoon,' I said. 'You're a cutie,' as I kissed one colleague on the cheek.

I turned to see him blush and attempt to remove the lipstick. I bounded onto the stage and kissed the cheeks of *all* the committee. Nick seemed most embarrassed though. I loved it.

'Now, where is he?' I asked.

'Where's who?' asked Carmen, who was holding a mic.

'Ah, there he is.' I stepped off the stage and went directly to a balding man in the front row. 'Hello darling,' I said, sitting on his knee. 'Are you the boss?'

From the response of the crowd, my boss didn't need to answer.

'Don't worry dear; this is probably going to be the most you'll have to suffer at my hand today.'

My boss didn't look convinced as I planted a big red kiss high on his forehead.

'As nice as this feels, I can't sit here all day.' I returned to the stage and nodded to Aidan.

The music started and I sang my first song. After the song, I chatted freely with the crowd. Picked out some of the more handsome men and stirred them relentlessly. I even threw in the info that I was given, all of which I already knew, and of course I added some material of my own.

'I have a surprise for you,' I announced. 'When I agreed to do your function, there was only going to be one of me. Now I have three more. Please welcome The Poncettes ...'

The music played and Shelby Wright, Tanya Hide and Sam Booka floated, smooched and caroused their way to the stage. When they had arrived, the music changed and we performed one of our fifteen-minute routines.

I won't bore you with the details of the company awards, but we enjoyed handing them out, having fun with each recipient that came on stage. We did a couple more routines and I closed off our part of the afternoon.

As I left the stage, my boss came on. 'Give a big hand to Prissy DuPonce,' he said, applauding heartily. 'You're very good. I actually enjoyed myself.'

'Honey,' I said, leaning into the microphone he was holding. 'When I'm good ... I'm great! But when I'm bad I'm fantastic!' (This is roughly how a friend of mine said it and I liked his version better, I only slightly adjusted it)

Everyone laughed.

'I'd also like to thank the committee for today's function,' continued my boss. 'I believe food and drink are available ... yes, I have been given the nod. Enjoy.'

The staff applauded and rose from their seats and headed to the rear of the room where the food and drinks were being served.

We performed two more numbers before retiring to the lounge upstairs.

'Can we come in?' came the voice following the knock.

Aidan let the committee in.

'How did you like the show?' I asked.

'It was fantastic,' replied Sally. 'Better than I expected.'

'Everyone is talking about it downstairs,' added Carmen.

'They're asking for photos.'

'They're what?' I was quite surprised.

'Yeah, they want pictures with you,' continued Carmen. 'Do you have to leave soon? Please come back downstairs. The staff will appreciate it.'

'Can you give us a moment?'

'Sure. We'll be outside.'

Aidan closed the door.

'Are you going to do it?' asked Dean.

'I know most of these people.' I started pacing the room, flapping my hands. 'I can't do it. What if someone recognises me?

'They don't know that Peter and Prissy are the same,' added Rory.

'Yeah ... but … I know these people. What if …'

Mick placed his finger on my lips. 'No buts, no what ifs. Let's give them what they want.' They gathered around me. 'What have you got to lose, hon?'

I moved away from them and paced the room once more. When I turned, they were all looking at me eagerly. 'Okay, let's do it,' I said. I began waving my hands furiously in front of my face. 'What have I said?'

We freshened up and stepped through the door. As we glided along the corridor, we collected the committee and swept into the throng below.

'Daaarlings,' I called, descending the stairs. The staff turned. 'Get your cameras ready, Madame DuPonce is back.'

I could see smiles everywhere as we mixed and mingled. We were handed glasses of wine and champagne. I only managed to take a few sips, as I was too busy posing with various people. We stayed downstairs for about an hour and finally returned to the lounge, committee in tow.

'We can't thank you enough for being here today,' said Sally.

'It was my pleasure dear.'

'I do have one question?' asked Sally.

'What's that dear?'

'I know we gave you information about people, but you seemed to know more,' she asked. 'How is that?'

'A girl never reveals her secrets,' I smiled and kissed her on the cheek.

She laughed and the committee left.

'I hope you all brought something comfortable to travel in?' I said as we went into the changing room.

The troupe acknowledged.

'I think for this event, and possibly others, leaving wig and make-up on might be an advantage. Especially for me.'

'That's true,' said Mick. 'If you have to travel this way, then so will we. It'll add to the mystery.'

'Here, here,' said Dean.

'Thanks, guys. Shall we change and get going? Aidan, can you bring the van around so we can get stuff packed?'

'Sure thing.'

'By the way, dinner's on me tonight. You're all invited back to our place when we leave here. You can change and shower there.'

'Sounds great. Thanks, Peter,' said Mick.

Aidan returned and we began to take our gear to the van. We made a couple of trips and I was stopped quite a few times. Eventually we made it out of the venue.

* * * * *

Back at home, Alex had drinks waiting for us.

'To a successful function gang,' toasted Aidan.

'Indeed,' I agreed, emptying my glass. 'You guys know where everything is. Knock yourselves out.'

I was changing when I heard the phone ring. 'It's for you, Pete,' Alex called upstairs.

'I'll take it up here. Hello?' picking up the receiver beside the bed.

'Peter, it's Sally.'

'Hi there,' I said croaking and coughing.

'How you feeling?' she asked.

'Better, thanks. How did this afternoon go?'

'It was great. I'm sorry you missed it.'

'Yeah, my apologies again for not being there.'

'You would've enjoyed it.'

'I'm sure I would've. How was the entertainment?'

'It went over like a charm. The staff insisted on having photos taken with Prissy.'

'I'm glad to hear you got photos.' I stifled a giggle. 'At least I can get an idea of how it went.'

'Will you be at work tomorrow?'

'I should be.'

'We'll catch up then.'

'See you at work.' I replaced the receiver and laughed.

'What were you laughing about?' asked Alex as I came into the kitchen.

'That was Sally.'

'From work?'

'Yeah.'

'What did she have to say?' asked Dean, entering the kitchen.

'She was telling me how much I'd missed this afternoon.'

'Ah.'

'I still had to fake being sick. It was hard not to laugh.'

'Are you going to tell them?' asked Dean, carrying a plate of nibbles to the lounge room.

'Are you going to tell who what?' asked Mick.

'I think Dean is referring to whether I'm going to tell work who Prissy is.'

'How do you think they'll take it?' asked Rory.

'It will be an interesting committee meeting.'

'Yes it will,' said Alex.

* * * * *

As I walked to my office, the day after the function, everyone was still talking about Prissy and the show. Even the gays in the office were excited and not bitchy, which was a first.

'So, did you find out who it was?' I heard one guy asking one of his friends.

'Honey, this one's very tight,' the other replied.

'I'm sure he is.' They both laughed. I chuckled as I moved on. 'So, who is it then?'

'I don't know,' replied the second, sounding frustrated. 'Don't you worry your pretty little head though, I *will* find out who it is.'

'You're such a mole.'

'You know I love rooting around.'

I moved on. *If only they knew.*

We had our final committee meeting that afternoon.

'It was fantastic,' opened Sally.

'It's a shame I wasn't in the audience. It sounded like a lot of fun,' I said.

'We actually went and saw Prissy last Saturday night too,' said Sally

'Did you?' I said, trying to act surprised.

'We heard she was performing, so we went and checked it out. Didn't Alex mention we were there?'

'He mentioned something in passing that you were there, but I was at my worst Saturday night.'

'She'd do great with a cabaret show anywhere.'

'Was she that good?'

'I think so,' said Carmen. 'Saturday night and yesterday.'

I smiled to myself.

'What are you smiling about?' asked Nick.

'I need to let you in on a secret.'

'What's that?'

'Didn't you think it strange that Prissy knew *so* much about you and the company?'

'How did you know she knew?'

I smiled again.

'You were Prissy's inside contact, weren't you?' asked Sally. 'She wouldn't tell us yesterday.'

I placed a piece of paper on the table and slid it to Sally. 'Whom did you give this to?'

Sally opened the note. 'I gave it to Prissy, personally.'

'Yes you did.'

Nick was thinking frantically, his brow furrowing. Suddenly he grinned.

'Ah, you've worked it out, Nick,' I said.

'Worked what out?' asked Carmen.

'I know who Madame Prissy DuPonce is,' said Nick proudly. 'And I don't believe it.'

'Who?' asked Sally.

'Who else would know so much about us?' he said.

'Anyone,' replied Carmen.

'Not to the detail that Prissy did,' added Nick.

'What are you saying, Nick?' asked Sally.

Nick sighed. 'Think about it,' laying hands palm up on the table. 'Peter *is* Prissy DuPonce.'

I smiled and nodded. Nick smiled too. Sally and Carmen were dumbfounded.

'That's not possible,' said Sally.

'Isn't it, daaarlings?' I said in Prissy's voice.

Sally and Carmen looked at me suddenly.

'I am Prissy DuPonce. I decided to do it when all the others said no.'

'Well I never,' said Carmen, sitting back in her chair.

'No wonder you were off 'sick' Monday and Tuesday,' said Sally. 'You didn't want us to know.'

'I've wanted to tell you for months, but decided to leave it as a surprise. Now you know. However, I'd prefer that no one else knows.'

'Okay,' they replied in unison.

'Not even my community know who Prissy is, well, not that I'm aware of.'

15. Christmas Changes

Christmas was upon us very quickly. New costumes, new routines. New shoes! My performances at RPs were going really well. The crowd gave me as much crap as I gave them. One night in particular, Peachy let me host for her so she could have a night off with her partner. I'd already teed up with RPs what needed to be said and I spent extra time trawling the weekly papers for material. I ended up doing the Governor on my own, as the crowds didn't seem to respond to the Poncettes as well as I'd hoped. As for the Buckingham, well, I think there was a part of Devon that was happy to be selling.

'Did you tell the guys to be here as well?' Alex asked as we walked into the Buckingham.

'Yes he did,' replied Mick. 'What's all this about?'

'Isn't it a bit early for Christmas drinks?' asked Rory.

We greeted the guys warmly. 'It's the twenty-second of December. Of course it's not too early. It's good to see you here,' I said.

'What's all this about?' asked Dean.

'You'll find out,' Alex replied.

Just as we began to sit down, Devon appeared with not only his lawyer, but our lawyer and accountant. Alex and I greeted them and indicated seats. With drink in hand, Devon stepped up to the bar.

'Thanks to everyone for being here this afternoon,' Devon began. 'It would be silly of me not to think that you are all wondering what the hell's going on. All the staff and performers, along with business folk, in a closed bar.'

Devon's staff nodded along with our troupe.

'I have some good news and some sad news.'

The Buckingham staff began to protest. Devon waved for quiet.

'I'll get the sad news over and done with first. I've decided to retire from the publican business and sell the Buckingham.'

'Devon!' gasped Vince, the bartender. 'You can't.'

'Yeah, you can't sell. The Buckingham won't be the same without you,' cried another.

'I'm not hanging around for this. I'm leaving.' Declared another staff member, firmly placing his drink on the bar and beginning to leave.

'Jeremy, please wait.' Jeremy stopped and returned to his colleagues. 'I know this is hard. I've worked with you all for quite a long time now. However, when it's time, it's time.' Devon took a large drink. 'All is not lost. I wish to announce that the Buckingham has been sold.'

Vince, who was leaning on the bar, almost hit it when his elbow unwittingly slipped. The look on his face said it all. His expression was confused between the shock of Devon retiring and then to hear that the Buckingham had already been sold.

'Boys, smile and be happy. Your new owners know this place and you know them.'

Vince looked over to where Alex and I stood. He inclined his head in our direction and I nodded in return. Vince smiled and raised his glass.

'It is my great pleasure to announce that Alex and Peter Long-Smith have purchased the Buckingham Hotel. A toast to Alex and Peter.' Devon raised his glass, which was enthusiastically followed.

Devon drew a table to the middle of the room and the lawyers laid out the contracts. In front of the Buckingham staff and my troupe, and other family and friends, Devon, Alex and I signed the contracts. One of the staff members took some photos, which later hung on the walls.

'You sly thing, Devon,' declared Vince. 'That's why you wouldn't tell me why you ordered all of this …' Vince jumped behind the bar and began to retrieve several bottles of fine champagne from the fridges.

'I'm sorry, Vince, but I really wanted to wait until we had everyone together.'

'Let me give you a hand,' said Jeremy, as he too jumped behind the bar.

As Vince and Jeremy gleefully popped the corks, the other staff members readied the glasses and began handing out the drinks.

'To the new owners of the Buckingham,' toasted Devon.

'To the new owners,' echoed the room.

'I'd like to toast Devon. May he enjoy his retirement and get to do the things he always wanted to do,' I toasted.

'To Devon.'

'Is the food ready, Bert?' queried Devon, waiting for his glass to be refilled.

'It had better be,' he replied, laughing.

'Then let's eat,' declared Devon.

Bert downed his glass and went to the kitchen. Moments later, he returned carrying a tray of goodies and placed it on a clothed table. 'Hey, can one of you guys give me a hand please?' he called to the staff in general.

Soon several more platters of Christmas fare were placed on the tables. Yes, we were celebrating the signing of the contracts to the Buckingham, but we were also celebrating Christmas.

'Happy Christmas, darling,' I said, when Alex and I had a quiet moment.

'Happy Christmas to you too, my love,' replied Alex.

* * * * *

Christmas and New Year came and went with its usual amount of festivity and work. We began to make the changes we wanted to the Buckingham. One night after more work at the Buckingham, Alex commented how I was looking tired, I agreed with him.

'I think I'm trying to do too much.'

'Really?'

'Bite me. I'm going to bed!'

Alex was probably lucky he wasn't around when I got up the next day. Whether by design or not, I had slept until ten. I was supposed to be at work at eight. 'Hello,' I said answering the phone.

'Ah, good you're up.'

'Why the hell didn't you wake me this morning?' I said angrily. 'You know I have to be at work at eight.'

'Calm down, sweetie. You need the rest,' responded Alex, apparently ignoring my outburst. 'I've rung work and told them you won't be in today ...'

'... but ...'

'... shoosh ...'

'... bu...'

'Listen for a change. I've rung work for you. I've also rung the doctor. You have an appointment with Shane at twelve-thirty and *NO* is not an option.'

'I have to go to work.'

'No, you don't. You're not indispensable.'

'I need to be at work.'

'Do I have to call the doctor at twelve-thirty to make sure you're there?'

'I'm going to work.'

'No you're not!' I'd never heard Alex be so forceful with me before. 'You're not well and I want you to find out why.'

'I've just been doing too much at the Buckingham. There are a lot of rooms to change and it was no easy feat realigning the stage either.'

'The boys can do that. Leave them instructions.'

'They won't do it right.'

'Peter, you're going to the doctor and that's final!'

I heard the phone slam down in my ear. I'd upset Alex. I wiped away the tears.

* * * * *

I arrived at the doctor's office as instructed; otherwise, life at home would be impossible. Especially after the way Alex had sounded on the phone. As I walked in and took a seat in front of Shane, our family doctor for the past eight years, he asked what he could do for me, but before I could reply he looked me up and down stating he could see what he might need to do for me.

He rose. 'This way. Shoes off.'

I stepped onto the scales he indicated. 'Not good. I reckon you're about 15kgs overweight.'

'Oh.' I was stunned. 'I thought I had been looking after myself.'

'How long have you had that cut on your arm?'

'About ten days, I think.'

'Hmmm. When was the last time you had a full blood analysis done?'

'Five years maybe.'

'Roll up your sleeve.' Shane checked my blood pressure and then proceeded to take several vials of blood from my arm.

'Do you really need that much?'

'You're pale, tired, overweight and not healing very well. Yes I need that much.'

'When do you want me to come back?'

'We should have the results in about ten days. We'll talk

then.'

I left the doctor's office feeling a little shattered. I don't remember my trip home, but I made it safely.

* * * * *

Just over a week later, I returned to the doctors with Alex insisting he was coming along.

Shane called me into his office. He also noticed that Alex was with me this time and beckoned him in as well. 'Ah good, you're both here.' He led us down the hall to his room. He sat on his side of the desk whilst we took seats opposite him. As we settled, he shuffled a few pages in my file. 'I was just having a look at your results. Interesting.'

'Oh?'

'Do you have any history of heart disease or diabetes in your family?'

'Heart disease? What's wrong?' I asked very nervously.

'Your heart seems quite fine. It was a routine question.'

'Well, I don't recall mum and dad saying anything. As to the diabetes, my grandfather had mature-age diabetes over twenty-five years ago. Wait, he died of a heart attack about twenty years ago.'

'That helps. Peter, you have Type-2 diabetes.'

'Oh.' I was surprised. When I looked at Alex, he was startled.

'You weren't expecting that diagnosis?' said Shane, looking up, hearing my surprise.

'Not really.'

'I thought he was just exhausted,' faltered Alex.

'I'm referring you to the Albert's diabetes clinic,' added Shane, as he wrote the referral. 'They'll be able to help you with a more detailed dietary program, exercise recommendations, medications and treatment. In the meantime, you can start by reducing the fat and sugar intake. There's nothing to be scared of. If you do it right, there's every chance you'll beat this thing quickly and keep it well under control.'

I sat silently.

'Are you okay, Peter?'

'It's a lot to take in right now.'

'Understandable.'

* * * * *

Alex didn't go to work that day and so we decided to have lunch at The Corset and Tassel. We arrived home, both still stunned by the news. I grabbed the mail on my way in and tossed it onto the dining table.

'What do we do now?' I asked.

'Don't look at me,' replied Alex.

I shot him an angry look. 'Did I ask for this to happen?'

'No you didn't.'

'Then why be a pratt?'

'I wasn't.'

I growled and got up and made some tea. We drank it in silence. 'Shane did say that I could start with diet and exercise.'

'What do we change?'

'He did say to start reducing the fat and sugar intake. We can find out what foods are the best for a diabetic and go from there. At least until I've been to the clinic at the hospital.'

'We can do that. I'll check the net and you have a look in the cupboard.'

'Okay.'

After an hour of fossicking online, Alex walked into the kitchen with several pieces of paper in one hand.

'Wha'd'ya find?' I queried

'Lots of interesting stuff. What did you find?'

'Lots of interesting stuff.'

Alex shook his head.

'I'm going to have a shower,' I said.

'I'll see what we've got for dinner.'

When I came back downstairs, Alex was sitting at the table with a look of bemused shock on his face. 'What's the matter?' I asked, standing behind him.

16. Indiscretions of the Past.

Alex indicated for me to sit down.

'Sweetie, you have me worried,' I said.

'I think you should be surprised rather than worried,' he replied.

'What's happened?'

'Well, whilst you were in the shower, there was a knock at the door,' Alex began to explain. 'I opened it to be greeted by a much younger version of you,' he concluded, looking directly at me.

'What do you mean a younger version of *me*?' I queried.

'You'd better come with me.' Alex rose, took me by the hand and led me to the lounge.

He walked in first and as I followed, I registered someone rising from the couch. I looked at the boy and almost fell over. Thankfully, Alex was there to support me. I couldn't believe my eyes. Standing there was a boy, no more than sixteen or seventeen, that looked almost exactly like me. The only things different were his blonde hair and fair skin, neither of which I have. His eyes, nose, mouth and facial structure were definitely mine.

'This must be a trick? Surely?' I queried, falteringly.

'It's no trick and my name is Nate Wittner,' Nate responded, holding out his hand.

I didn't return the greeting, as I was feeling overcome. Alex helped me to a chair and I sat and stared at Nate. I didn't know what to do.

'Would you like to hear my story?' he ventured.

'That might be a good place to start,' responded Alex. 'Would you object if I recorded it? I have a feeling we'll need to hear it again after tonight.'

'I've gone one better for you,' he replied. He reached for his backpack, removed a folder, and handed it to Alex. 'I've gone over this on a regular basis and when I finished my year eleven exams last November, I updated it to the present. It's a complete version of events.'

'Thanks,' responded Alex, taking the folder.

'Would you still like to hear it for yourselves?'

'Let me get some coffee first. Would you like one?' offered Alex.

'Do you have tea?'

'We do. How do you like it?'

'With milk and sugar, thank you.'

'I'll have a double scotch, straight, please,' I added.

Alex left the room to fetch the drinks.

'This must be a shock for you?' asked Nate, after a few minutes of awkward silence.

'Just a little,' I replied, nervously.

'I'm just glad to be away from Adelane.'

'Is that where you're from?'

'Yeah. I'll wait for the other guy to come back before I give you the full story.'

'Okay.'

We sat in silence for a few more minutes. Alex handed me my drink and I sculled it down in one gulp. Even Alex looked at me with surprise. Alex gave Nate his tea and then sat down himself in the other chair to listen to the tale.

For the next two hours, Nate gave a run down on his life

and how he got to be sitting in our lounge that January evening. He was born in Adelane, just over sixteen and a half years ago and had his mother's maiden name. His mum, alone, no father, raised him.

When he was eleven, his mother met a man who eventually moved in with them. His mum became pregnant, although miscarried. From that time on, Nate's stepfather – as his mum eventually married him – began to distance himself from Nate. When he was thirteen, his mum had another baby and another when he was fourteen. This only served to exclude Nate increasingly from the new family life.

At that time, Nate decided to take control of his own life. He studied hard and discovered that he could get what he wanted, all he had to do was ask. By now, he was *encouraged* to stay in his reasonably self-contained section of the house. He only joined the rest of the family for meals. His mum would spend time with him, but her husband, requiring her to attend to one of the other children, to which she always relented, usually interrupted it. Nate stressed that he was never abused physically or sexually, but we knew and told him that the isolation and apparent neglect was equally regarded as abuse, it was mental rather than physical.

Having said that, Nate never came across as suffering. He seemed very balanced. He was proud of his scholastic achievements and although he could get what he wanted, he soon set himself goals for which he rewarded himself with various items; such as a new laptop, music players, phones and books.

When Nate was sixteen, his mum had another baby and after that, he rarely saw his mum or stepsiblings. He decided to search out his biological father, but had to wait until after his exams to do anything seriously. In the meantime, he did ask his mum about whom his father was, only to be told that he was gay and wouldn't want to know him.

This actually disturbed Nate and made him even more

determined to find his real father. As soon as his exams were finished, he began his search. Nate obtained a copy of his birth certificate and the name of his father, Peter Long, was written on it. Whether in the hope that his mum would be able to reunite or not, Nate wasn't sure, but there it was. He was happy he had somewhere to start. That night, Nate used his social networking account to see if his dad was there. After half an hour of searching through the long list of matches to *Peter Long*, he came across my profile. At first, Nate said he was confused as the surname was actually showing as Long-Smith, but the picture attached was unmistakable. He held up a photo of his own next to that of mine on the screen and decided I was his father.

He saw that I lived in Melvegas and soon as Christmas and New Year was over, he'd packed his bags and travelled to look for me. Once he arrived, he checked into a backpacker's hostel and searched through the phone directory for a Peter Long-Smith. His search came back with a Peter Long and mine. Nate said he decided to take the punt and try mine first, because of the surname from his network site.

He found our address and watched me come and go for a couple of days before plucking up the courage to knock on our door. Now, here he was, sitting on my couch, telling this extraordinary tale. If he didn't look so much like me, I would've asked him to leave very early on.

'That's about it,' he concluded. 'I've probably gone into more details in the file, but you'll find the story is the same.'

'You've thought about this?' asked Alex.

'Quite a lot,' Nate replied. 'I decided that if my mother wasn't going to love me the way she should, then perhaps my father would.'

'You'll be eighteen in a year or so, surely it wouldn't matter as much?' queried Alex.

'Whether I'm sixteen, twenty-six or thirty-six, I want my

parents to be proud of me and vice-versa.'

'Consider yourself told, Alex,' I interjected, smiling wryly.

'Ah, welcome back, Peter,' responded Alex.

'I'm going to need time to digest all this information, Nate. I trust you understand?'

'I do. My mobile number is in the file,' he replied. 'Give me a call if you want any more information.'

'We'll do that,' I said. 'You do realise that Alex and I are gay and partnered?'

'Yeah, I sort of worked that out,' he replied, smiling.

'That doesn't bother you?' asked Alex.

'It might take some getting used to, but if I am to be with my real father, that'll just have to be part of who he is.'

'Like I said,' I added, rising from my chair, 'I'll need time to digest all this information. I will give you a call.'

'Thanks,' said Nate.

'Can we give you a lift back to your hostel?' asked Alex.

'It's okay, I can catch a cab,' replied Nate.

'Would you like another cup of tea, while you wait?' I asked, feeling a bit more like myself again.

'It's fine, I'll wait out front for the cab.'

Alex and I escorted Nate to the front door and watched as he leant against our front gate and called for a cab. We went back to the lounge and collapsed on the couch.

'What just happened?' I asked.

'I have no idea,' replied Alex. 'You never told me you had a kid.'

'I didn't know I had one, if he is even mine.'

'Unless he's a freak of nature, there's no mistaking who he looks like.'

'There is that.'

'Do you remember ever sleeping with a woman for this to happen?'

I sat there and thought long and hard. 'Nope, nothing comes to mind about me doing anything like that so long ago.'

'Don't forget to add nine months.'

'Oops, I forgot about that. Let me think again. When was he born?'

'I don't think he told us specifically.'

'What about the file?' I picked it up and opened it to the first page. 'Ah, here it is, April 12 So, he'll be seventeen next birthday, go back from there and add a further nine months. That would make it around July, the time I moved to Melvegas.'

'Which was before you met me.'

'Yes and I know I've only been with you since then and certainly not with a woman.'

'That's good to hear,' Alex said, smiling and hugging me. 'So, what happened when you left?'

'That's sooo long ago, I don't know if my memory will stretch that far.'

'You're not *that* old.'

We laughed.

'Okay, July ... July ... July ... got it. That was when I had my going away which was combined with Vaughan's engagement party. I'll give him a call tomorrow and see what he remembers. What is Nate's mother's name?'

'Alex grabbed the file this time and flicked it open. Sally Wittner, he's written here.'

'Sally Wittner, I don't remember a girl by that name,' I reflected. 'Perhaps Vaguey will remember.'

* * * * *

Just after lunch, with Nate's file in front of me, I called Vaughan.

'Hey, Vaguey,' I greeted, when he answered the call.

'How's it going little brother?'

'Confusing.'

'Hmm, should I be surprised?'

'Very funny. This is for real.'

'What's up?' he asked.

'Do you remember a Sally Wittner?'

'Let me see, Sally Wittner.' The phone went quiet for a moment. 'Yeah, she was in my class at school. She also had the hots for you, if I remember right.'

'Oh my god, *that* Sally Wittner. How could I forget her?'

'What's she done to you?'

'That's what I'm trying to work out. Was she at the party we had for your engagement and my farewell? I don't remember, I think I drank a little too much that night.'

'I think we all did that night. Let's see, I'll check with Coralie. Hang on.'

'Okay.'

I heard a muttered conversation in the background.

'I knew Coralie'd remember. No, Sally wasn't at the party. If anything, she was the most deliberate exclusion.'

'Oh?'

'She wasn't really that well liked and had tried to get every guy she knew into bed. You, apparently, were at the top of her list as you were gay. Coralie remembers us all going to a bar after the party where we happened to run into Sally. As we were already a little drunk, we told her what you were doing. Coralie remembers Sally buying you drinks most of the night. All I can assume is that she got you so drunk that you wouldn't remember a thing the next day.'

'If that's true, then what happened last night might indeed be true.'

'What happened last night?'

I quickly recapped Nate's story for Vaughan.

'No way,' he replied. 'You dirty little boy,' he added, sniggering.

'That's enough out of you. This is serious,' I stated.

'I know, Petey, but you have to admit it ridiculously hilarious?'

'I guess so.'

'What are you going to do?'

'The only thing I can do, ask for a paternity test. I'll see what the results are and go from there.'

'Will Nate agree to that?'

'If he wants to know the truth, he will.'

'Good luck, little brother.'

'Thanks.'

'Don't forget to tell him that he looks almost exactly like you, except for the blonde hair and fair skin,' Alex suddenly added.

'Thanks, Alex. Are you for real, Petey? When do we get to meet him?' queried Vaughan.

'You, in the other room, get off the phone,' I yelled at Alex. 'Vaughan, hang on a minute, I don't even know if he's mine yet.'

'I'll keep you updated. Talk again soon,' confirmed Alex.

I walked into the kitchen. 'You, really have to stop listening into other's people conversations over the phone.'

'Oh, sweetie, you love me,' was his reply.

'That's beside the point.'

'Have you rung the doctor yet?'

'For what?'

'To book in for that paternity test?'

'I haven't spoken to Nate about that yet.'

'Book it for Monday and if he says no, you can cancel. If he agrees, you won't have to wait further.'

'Yes, I do love you.'

Alex smiled and tapped his cheek. I kissed him accordingly. I walked back to the dining room and duly booked in to see my doctor on Monday afternoon.

'Honey?' Alex called from the kitchen.

'What's up?' I replied going in to see him.

'Would you like to invite Nate over for lunch tomorrow? You can ask him about having the paternity test, as well as get to know him further.'

'That might be nice, but I'm also reticent about getting his hopes up in case I'm not his father.'

'Oh, sweetie, I don't think that's going to happen. Freaks of nature don't look that much alike.'

'Perhaps.'

17. Parenting

Let me jump forward a week. We had an enjoyable lunch with Nate and he was happy to have the paternity test. I guess I wasn't that surprised when I received the result to say that the match between us was likely to be 98.997%.

Nate was slightly more excited than I was, as I was still digesting all the information. He wanted to come and stay immediately, but I had to slow him down, as I needed to discuss the outcome with Alex. He was naturally disappointed but I promised I'd ring him the following day to let him know what was going to happen.

I walked into the house and strolled into the dining room, dropped my satchel on the sideboard and went in to the kitchen. I foraged around in the fridge for a few minutes, oblivious to the fact that Alex was standing at the sink, looking at me.

I stood up from the fridge, sandwich items in my hand and walked over to the bench.

I heard the polite cough emanate from the other side of the kitchen. I turned to see a bemused Alex looking at me.

'What?' I asked.

'Am I no longer privy to medical information pertaining to your royal personage?' he asked mockingly supercilious.

'I'm sorry, sweetie, I was in another world,' I replied.

'So I noticed,' he said. 'What's the result?'

'I have a son,' I said simply, walking over to him.

He reached out and hugged me.

'I have a son,' I repeated.

'I heard you the first time, sweetie.'

'I know, but I still can't believe it.' I released Alex from my hug and wiped a tear from my eye.

'Where is he, then?'

'I told him I needed to talk to you about it first.'

'What's there to talk about?'

'It's a big decision,' I insisted, collecting my sandwich and heading to the lounge.

Alex sat beside me. 'What's there to talk about? He's *your* son. A boy needs his father and after what he's told us, he needs his father more than ever before.'

'It sounds like he's your son, not mine. Ours, I should say.'

'Thank you, sweetie,' Alex said. 'He'll always be your blood.'

'He will be our son, even though there'll be no missing exactly whose he is.'

'What do we do now?'

'Get a room ready, I suppose,' I said. 'I have a son,' I said once more and then really broke down in Alex's arms.

'We need to celebrate,' said Alex, rising from the couch and leaving the lounge room.

I heard the popping of a cork and soon Alex returned with two glasses and a bottle of champagne. 'Here's to new adventures. When did you say we'd collect him?'

'I told him I'd call him tomorrow with an answer.'

'No you're not, you're going to call him now,' Alex insisted.

'Surely it can wait?'

'Are you kidding, you know damn well you want to call him right now!'

'I do, but I don't want to be hasty.'

'Bollocks. Make the bloody call, or I will.' Alex handed me

the phone.

I dialled Nate's number and gave him the news. He was ecstatic. He was even more excited when I told him we'd collect him that night.

Two hours later, we were carrying Nate's bags into our house, which was now to become his home. We all cleaned out the second room and Alex and I left Nate to unpack. We went into the kitchen to make hot drinks.

'Right,' I said, leaning on the doorframe, leading to the kitchen. 'I have something I want to discuss with you.'

'What have you done this time?' Alex said.

'Excuse me, it's nothing wrong!'

'What is it, hon?'

'Since taking over the Buckingham, Prissy's shows, my diabetes and now discovering I have a son, I've been thinking whether it's time to leave work.'

'Why do you want to do that?'

'The shows are going very well and need planning. The Buckingham is getting busier and I think that at least one of us should be seen there more often. My diabetes has added variations to our eating and exercise habits. Now we have Nate to care for. Perhaps one of us needs to be around to ensure we do that to the best of our ability.'

Alex stood, deep in thought. 'I think you might be right. Perhaps that is something you could do.'

'We can talk about it over the weekend and see how we're feeling the more we think about it?' I suggested.

'Is there much more that needs to be thought about?' Alex said, stroking his chin and looking official. 'You've stated the reasons most eloquently.'

'Pffft, don't get snooty.'

Alex laughed. 'Sweetie, it's a great idea. I'd do it myself but I think I'd get bored not working.'

'That's what I thought for a while too, but when I factor in how much time Madame DuPonce is requiring, I'll never be bored.'

'Then there's the Buckingham, and Nate.'

'Then there's the Buckingham, and Nate, and the diabetes,' I said.

'I guess we'll need to draw down some funds from the inheritance,' suggested Alex.

'What inheritance?' said the voice from across the dining rom.

Peter turned to see Nate crossing the room.

'When Alex's Aunt Nedelina died, she left him everything. No one else in the family got a cent.'

'So I'm a rich kid now?' asked Nate.

'We'll see about that,' said Peter. 'It's earned, not just given.'

'Alex had it given to him,' said Nate.

'Yes I was,' said Alex, 'but there was more to it than that.'

Nate looked at Alex.

'Peter and I have been together for fifteen years now,' said Alex. 'I was always Aunt Nede's favourite nephew and when she died, it was clearly stated in her will why she did what she did. Simply put, I, and Peter as my partner, was the only niece or nephew who'd had the longest relationship. We were also the only same sex couple. She liked the way we'd work out our problems rather than just walk away and separate, not that I ever wanted to do that to Peter anyway. As a result, we got her fortune.'

'Am I allowed to know how much?' asked Nate.

'I don't like to talk about it,' said Alex.

'Neither do I,' added Peter. 'It sits there, earns interest and now and then we draw some of it for what we need. Otherwise, we've both still worked so don't need that money specifically.'

'I'd still like to know, but I guess I'll just have to wait.'

'Exactly,' said Peter.

'So, do we need to draw any funds down or not?' asked Alex.

'Let's not rush into that yet,' I replied. 'Prissy and the Buckingham seem to be filling our coffers well enough.'

'True.'

'I'll tell work on Monday.'

'How will they take it?'

'Not well I suspect, but it's not like people haven't resigned in the past.'

'Who's not going to take what well?' said Nate.

'My work, when I tell them I'm resigning,' I replied.

'Why are you resigning?'

'To look after you.'

'Hey, I don't need that much looking after,' Nate replied.

'Oh, I see. Now it's all going to be about you is it?' I said.

Nate look mortified and I couldn't hold back any longer.

'That was cruel,' said Alex, pushing past me carrying a tray of drinks. 'He's going to have to get used to our humour and we're going to have to get used to the fact that we just can't speak out as loudly as we used to.'

'Nor walk around naked,' I added.

Nate made as if he was going to throw up and then laughed.

'On second thoughts, that won't take as long as I thought,' Alex said, placing the tray on the table.

* * * * *

The first few days were awkward and exciting. Saturday lunch was a much more relaxed affair. No one had to be up at a specific time to be anywhere and so we all took our time doing whatever it was we needed to do.

'Can I ask you a question, Peter, I mean Dad ... what am I going to call you?' asked Nate, as he made his sandwich for lunch.

'Sure. What is it? Call me what you feel most comfortable with.'

'I'm going to try for Dad,' he replied smiling. 'Where were

you last night?'

'I didn't know you knew I'd gone out,' I replied smiling.

'I came down later in the evening and only saw Alex in the lounge. He was on the phone, so I didn't disturb him.'

I smiled and hung my head. 'I guess I can tell you where I was. I'm a drag queen. I was performing last night.'

Nate almost choked on his lunch and was embarrassed when he spat it out on the table. 'I'm sorry, I didn't mean to be so rude.'

'It's okay,' I said. 'I probably should've waited until you'd finished your mouthful.'

'You're a drag queen?' asked Nate, having regained his composure.

'Yeah. I created her last year when I needed an act for my work's Christmas function,' I explained.

'Can I come and watch sometimes?' he asked enthusiastically.

'We'll see,' I said.

After lunch, the three of us did the grocery shopping. Begrudgingly, Nate came with us, as we weren't ready to leave him at home alone.

'Why do you have to be careful what you eat, Dad?' he asked as we chose more diabetic friendly foods.

'I'm a diabetic and have to watch what I eat,' I explained. 'Is there anything you'd like to have?'

'What do you mean?'

'Food. Is there something you particularly like to eat?'

'Uhm, peanut butter sandwiches.'

'Done,' I said.

'Really?' I could hear the surprise in Nate's voice.

'Yes, really,' I encouraged. 'You okay with that, Alex?'

'More than okay,' he replied. 'However …'

'Here's the catch,' said Nate, looking down again.

'All I was going to suggest was not every week,' he said. 'That's all.'

'Okay.' Nate smiled again.

'This is what we'll do,' I added. 'Nate, you always get to choose the bread you want and the peanut butter you want, neither of which Alex or I will be allowed to touch. It'll be all yours. So, if you eat it all in two days, you'll have to wait until the next time we go shopping.'

'Am I allowed to change what I have on the bread?' he asked.

'You can have whatever you want.'

We continued in silence, collecting the things we needed.

'Aren't you going to ask more about my life in Adelane?' asked Nate as we walked back to the car.

'No,' I said simply. 'As much as we'd like to know, our aim is to make a happy place for you to live in. Besides, your file was pretty comprehensive.'

As we drove home, I caught a glimpse of Nate in the rear view mirror wiping a tear from his eye. 'Are you okay, Nate?'

'Yeah. I'm just happy to be here with the two of you, especially with my father,' Nate explained.

Nate excused himself and went to his room once we'd unpacked the car. The house was quiet until Alex and I began getting dinner ready. Surprisingly, Nate appeared to offer his help.

'How are you at peeling vegies?' I asked.

'Shit,' he replied.

'Good. Be shit with these,' I laughed and handed him the sweet potatoes, carrots, a peeler and a knife.

Nate told us at dinner that he was looking forward to going to school. 'I think I'll do music this year,' Nate said at dinner.

'Do you play an instrument?' I asked.

'I prefer to sing, although I did start learning the piano when I was younger,' he added.

'There's a very old piano in the back room you're welcome to use,' said Alex.

'Maybe,' said Nate smiling.

18. Who is the Mysterious Bidder?

Towards the end of February, I was at the Buckingham sorting through administrative stuff and having some lunch. When I'd finished, I went outside and saw some workers placing a sign on the building next door.

I crossed the road to look at the signage. 'Interesting,' I commented to myself. Grabbing my mobile phone, I dialled the contact number.

'This is Harry,' came the strong male voice.

'Hi, my name's Peter Long-Smith,' I said. 'I've just seen a sign go up on a building next to the Buckingham Hotel. How soon before we can get a look inside?'

'Nice to meet you, Peter,' replied Harry. 'We've only been handed the keys today. How soon would you like to view the property?'

'Tomorrow morning?'

'Let me check my schedule. I usually only do business on weekdays.'

'I understand, except my partner works regular hours, and weekends would be the best time for us to view such a property.'

'I can appreciate that. How does ten a.m. sound?'

'We can do that. Do you have any other information about the property? Like price, any valuations and the like?'

'I think we received some of those as well today. I will

bring what I can tomorrow.'

'That'd be great. See you at ten.' I terminated the call and stood and looked at the building. 'Shit, what have I done?'

* * * * *

Dinner that night was interesting. 'So how was everyone's day?' I asked.

'I'm glad it's Friday,' reported Alex.

'I hate school,' grumped Nate.

'I see,' I said, having to curb my enthusiasm slightly.

'What about you, hon?' asked Alex.

'I'm glad you asked. I had a great day,' I replied.

'Indeed. What did you do?'

'We have an appointment to view a property tomorrow morning at ten.'

'What!' exclaimed Alex.

'We have an appointment to view a property tomorrow morning at ten.'

'I heard you the first time.'

'Then why'd you ask?'

Alex growled at me. Nate sniggered.

'Enough from you,' snapped Alex.

'Don't take it out on Nate. It's not his fault you had a crap day at work.'

Alex shot one of his dagger looks at me. I poured more wine into his glass. Nate tried for some as well.

'We've talked about that young man,' I said, refusing to fill his glass, with anything other than the juice that was already on the table.

'I had to try,' he responded, smiling.

'Perhaps I should explain,' I said.

'Perhaps,' Alex responded tetchily.

'Why do you want to have a look at this building, dad?' asked Nate.

'As you know, Alex and I own the Buckingham Hotel. This building happens to be next door. I've always wanted to have an entertainment venue that allows for more options than a hotel can provide.'

Nate looked at Alex.

'Yes, he's talked about this before, but we've never been able to follow up on it or found the right place,' explained Alex.

'Until now,' I said enthusiastically.

'What's the building like?' asked Alex.

'It's a three storey building. There are three shops at street level. A café's in one and the others are currently vacant. I couldn't tell if the first and second floors were occupied, but by the looks of them, I'd say they're also vacant.'

'I see.'

'We'll know more tomorrow.'

'Is that your mobile or mine sweetie?' asked Alex.

'Mine,' I replied, listening to the ring. 'Be right back.'

'That's not good,' I said, placing my mobile on the dining table.

'What's wrong?' asked Alex.

'We can't view the building until Tuesday,' I said. 'The call was from Harry, the agent. He's required to assist with some auctions tomorrow and won't be available. I'll have to look through the property myself.'

'That's okay,' encouraged Alex. 'You're the one with the ideas. You'll know if it's worthwhile or not.'

'I really wanted you two to be there.'

'You have a look first. If it's right, you can show us through.'

'Okay.'

* * * * *

The shows kept me busy, but I was still nervous until the following Tuesday when I'd get to see the property. *What would it be like? Would we be able to afford it? Duh, I reminded myself, we had the inheritance. Would the building be big enough?* The questions rolled repeatedly in my mind.

I dumped my stuff in my office at the Buckingham and waited outside the property next door, wandered into the café and was pleased to see it busy. I grabbed a coffee and went back outside. Harry was waiting for me.

He showed me through the two vacant shops at street level. They shared rear access with the café and I could see potential already. We went upstairs and looked through the large spaces on the first and second floors.

'Impressive,' I said. 'I see all sorts of things fitting in here.'

'Like what?' asked Harry.

'This floor will probably be turned into a rehearsal space,' I explained, looking out of the windows of the third floor. 'The one below I'd like to turn into a showroom.'

'Showroom?' asked Harry.

'Dinner theatre type of showroom,' I responded.

'Ah.'

We concluded the viewing and I waited as Harry locked the property.

'Is it what you were hoping for?' asked Harry.

'Very much. It'll need some work and we'll probably want to get an independent valuation. Is it possible to have first option of the purchase, pending valuation outcomes?'

'That's possible. I'll leave appropriate notes on the file at the office.'

'Thanks. We'll let you know as soon as we can.' Harry and I shook hands and I went into the Buckingham.

* * * * *

'How'd it go today?' asked Alex at dinner.

'It went very well,' I replied. 'We have first option on purchase. I suggested we'd get a valuation done.'

'When?' asked Alex, between mouthfuls.

'This Friday and we'll get the report the following Tuesday,' I answered.

'That's quick.'

'I think he realised how quickly we needed it. Thankfully we have first option so we're safe for the moment.'

'Let's hope it's good.'

* * * * *

Tuesday arrived. The day we were to get the valuation. I spent a frustrating morning trying to work on some new ideas for Prissy. I decided to take a walk along the street where the Buckingham was located.

'Hello?' I said, answering my mobile.

'It's Gary Nicholls from Nicholls, Slater & Thomas.'

'How are you?'

'Well, thank you. I have the valuation report for you. Can I drop by?'

'I'm not in my office right now, but I will be there in about fifteen minutes.'

'It'll take me about thirty to get to you.'

'See you then. The side door should be open. I'll meet you in the bar.' I walked back to the office and waited for Gary to arrive. I paced back and forth around the bar.

'Will you sit down and drink this!' said a frustrated Vince, placing a scotch and coke on the bar.

'I can't,' I said. 'This meeting will determine if we buy the building next door.'

'Talk to me.'

I described the building, the shops, the vacant floors and the ideas I had.

'Wow.'

Gary walked through the door and I greeted him warmly. We went to my office and talked for an hour about the valuation.

'I trust it's what you wanted to hear.'

'Yes and no,' I smiled.

Gary looked at me oddly.

'Well, yes, because it's a sound property and won't need a lot of work to change it to what we plan for it. And no, because it's a huge task now to change the building to what we want.'

'Fair enough.'

'I'm grateful for your help once again,' I said rising.

'I'm always happy to assist,' replied Gary, returning my handshake. I showed him through the bar.

'What's the verdict?' asked Vince, as I closed the door behind Gary.

'The verdict on what?' I replied as innocently as I could.

'On the valuation,' replied Vince, the smile curling at the corner of his lips.

'What makes you say I had a valuation done on anything?'

'The guy you just showed out, he came and did the valuation on this place before you guys bought it,' responded Vince. 'And the fact that you told me while you were waiting for him to arrive.'

'Ah. You remembered.'

'Yes I did. I was the one who had to let him in to do the valuation for here.'

'And people wonder why we pay you what we do.'

Vince blushed.

'Don't get me wrong, we're very grateful.'

'Thanks, Peter. Does that mean I'm getting a raise?'

'Ah ... no.'

'Damn.' Vince walked away, lightly punching the bar with his hand.

* * * * *

I went back to my office and sat down, the valuation in my hand. I picked up the phone. 'Harry? Peter Long-Smith here.'

'Peter, good to hear from you.'

'I'm calling about the property.'
'What would you like to know?'
'How much is being asked?
'2.5 million.'
'Okay. We're definitely interested.'
'I'll let the vendor know.'
'Before I go, can we make a time to have another look through the building?'
'How about four-thirty tomorrow afternoon?'
'Done.' I hung up the phone.

* * * * *

'I have some good news,' I announced at dinner that night.
'What is it?' asked Alex.
'We got the valuation today.'
'How was it?' asked Alex.
'About what we expected.'
'That good huh?'
I smiled. 'Structurally it's quite sound and only needs minor engineering work. Remember, we had given the valuer a good idea of what we intended to use the premises for and so he was able to value it accordingly.'
'So we can do what we want?'
'Pretty much.'
'Can we have another look at it?'
'Yes. Tomorrow afternoon at four-thirty.'
'Do you want me to wait at the hotel?' asked Nate.
'You're coming with us.'
Nate looked surprised. 'Why?'
'You're a part of this family, Nate, your old enough to be involved,' said Alex.
'If we're successful, it'll mean more time working and I don't want it to get in the way of us looking after you,' I added.
'I've had to cope with worse,' Nate said.

* * * * *

After dinner the following night, when we had all viewed the property, Nate excused himself to study and Alex and I did the dishes.

'Have you asked for a price yet?' asked Alex, as he stacked away the last of the pots.

'The vendor wants $2.5 million for the building.'

'How much work do we have to do on it?'

'I reckon all up, with what needs to be done, plus the sort of fit-out we want to do, we'll need to spend up to a million.'

'Sounds fair, though I hope we spend much less.'

'So do I,' I echoed. 'I was thinking we'd offer $2 million, due to the minor engineering work required, but we don't go above $2.2 million.'

'I like that idea. Why don't you set up a time to meet the vendor at the estate agents office and we can discuss the options?'

'I will. Should we meet with the accountant first?'

'Might be an idea to include her on this deal as well,' replied Alex. 'I'll call her tomorrow.'

We met with the accountant at Alex's work at one o'clock Monday afternoon. She was happy with our plans and gave us further advice for negotiating a fair price.

* * * * *

I rolled over lazily in bed and began to hug Alex. I wasn't perturbed when he moved and got out of bed quickly. I was astounded when I heard the word, 'Shit' emanate from his mouth a few times.

I woke up quickly. 'What's the matter?'

'It's eight-thirty!'

'It can't be.'

'Look at the clock then,' said Alex a little angrily.

'So it is.'

'Don't get smart. I'll be late for work and Nate'll be late for school.'

'No he won't.'

'Yes ... he ... will.'

'No .. he .. won't. It's school holidays.'

'When did they start?'

'This week.'

'Whooy dirn't yooo shet the ararm?' called Alex between mouthfuls of toothpaste.

'What did you say?'

'I said – why didn't you set the alarm?'

'Ah. I thought yours was on.'

'We got up okay yesterday and Monday?'

'Much to Nate's disgust. We had places to be when you went to work.'

Alex rushed downstairs. 'I don't have time for a coffee. I'll see you tonight.'

He kissed me on the cheek and was out the door.

I made some breakfast and sat down to look at my list. 'I'll give Harry a call once I've had a shower.'

By the time I came back downstairs, Nate was up and seemed to have half the pantry on the kitchen bench.

'I gather you're not that hungry today?'

'Nah, just a light snack.' He chuckled.

'What are you doing today?'

'Nothing really. Probably just eat and hang around.'

'A normal day then.' I smiled. 'We're going shopping after lunch.'

'Do I have to?' whined Nate.

'Now you do.'

Nate hung his head and left the kitchen.

'I'll let you ride in the baby seat if you want to?' I laughed as I heard Nate's groan emanate from the lounge.

I was startled when the phone rang just as I was about to pick it up. 'Hello?'

'Good morning, Peter, Harry here.'

'Hey, Harry. How's it going?'

'Not too bad. I have some news about the property.'

'Oh?'

'Whilst we said you could have first option, a colleague accepted an offer from another party, not knowing of the standing arrangement.'

'Oh. When did this happen?'

'This morning.'

'Can I ask how much and who it was?'

'Who, no. That remains private.'

'Okay.'

'As to how much, they've offered $2 million.'

'Right. We'll offer $2.1 million. Did you speak to the other party yourself?'

'As I said, a colleague took the call as I was actually talking to the vendor.'

'How does that affect our first option?'

'I was in the process of making the adjustments on the computer file when the offer was listed. Unfortunately, it can't be changed now. I'm sorry about that Peter.'

'Stuff happens. We'll just have to make sure we bid higher. Keep me informed.'

'I will.'

'Right then,' I said wandering into the lounge room. 'That puts a bit of a dampener on things. I'd better ring Alex.'

'What's the matter?' asked Nate.

'Someone's made a bid on the property already.'

'I thought you said you had first option?'

'So did I, but the agent hadn't updated the file quickly enough and now someone else has made a bid.'

'Bummer.'

'Very much so.' I picked up my mobile and dialled Alex's number. 'Hmm, engaged.'

'Aren't you going to leave a message?'

'Nah, he'll see he got a missed call from me.'

I walked into the kitchen and opened the pantry door, not really concentrating on a grocery list.

'Phone, Peter,' called Nate.

I rushed to pick it up, 'Peter Long-Smith here.'

'Peter, it's Harry.'

'You have some news?'

'The other party has made a further bid.'

'And?'

'$2.15 million.'

'I see. Then we bid $2.2 million.'

'Okay, I'll enter it in.'

I disconnected from Harry and went back to the pantry.

'Staring at it won't fill it up.'

'Huh? What?'

'Staring at the pantry won't fill it up again.'

'My mind was elsewhere.'

'Really. I never would've guessed. What's wrong now?'

'You will be riding in the baby seat if you don't watch out. The phantom bidder has made another bid.'

'Perhaps you should go down to the agent and make a firm bid that can't be beaten?'

'Maybe we should do that. Go and get ready, we'll go to the agent, have some lunch and then do the shopping.'

'It's the holidays.'

'And?'

'Do I have to go?' whinged Nate.

'Yes!'

Forty-five minutes later, we were walking into the offices of the agent. As I waited for Harry, Alex turned up. He was just hanging up his mobile as he entered the agents.

'What are you doing here?' he asked.

'I could ask you the same thing?' I questioned.

'Can I help you?' asked the receptionist.

'I'm here to see Queenie,' he replied.

'We're dealing with Harry,' I said.

Just then, Harry and Queenie entered the front office.

'Hi, Peter,' greeted Harry with a handshake.

'Hey, Harry,' I responded. 'You remember my partner, Alex?'

'Yes.' Harry shook Alex's hand.

'I'm Queenie,' she said approaching Alex. 'This is the bidder I was telling you about just now.'

'Excuse me?' stated Harry. 'We really do need to do something about those privacy issues.'

'What do you mean?' I asked.

'Come into my office and I'll explain.'

'This'll be good,' said Nate as he followed along behind.

'I want you to sit in a corner a stay quiet,' I turned, whispering to him.

'I know this. I just want to listen.'

Harry showed us seats. 'Where do we begin? For me it began when I spoke with you this morning, Peter, and told you that another bid had been made.'

'That was the one I entered about nine-thirty when I took a call from Alex,' added Queenie.

'So you're the mystery bidder?' I said.

'Me? That would make you my mystery bidder.'

'Queenie and I have just been speaking and we compared the names of those bidding. We can see but we're not allowed to divulge the information to others. It's only just now that I've discovered that you two have been bidding against each other all morning.'

I sat dumbfounded. I turned sharply when I heard Nate chuckling. 'I thought I told you to be quiet!'

'I'm sorry, but it's funny,' he replied, and laughed a bit more.

It was true. Alex and I had been bidding against each other all morning. The more I thought about it, the funnier it became. I started to laugh. 'Well, wha'd'ya know, after fifteen years together, we still can't communicate properly.'

Alex began to laugh. 'We were a bit rushed this morning and didn't get a chance to talk about what we'd do.'

'Which we should've done last night,' I added. 'We're sorry, Harry, we didn't realise what was happening. What was the last bid made and who made it? If you can tell us that now we know we were both bidding.'

The phone buzzed on Harry's desk. 'Harry here ... right, I see. I'll come out and have a look ... he is, is he? ... this is interesting. Thank you.' He returned the handset. 'If you'll excuse me, the receptionist has opened a letter with yet another offer for the property and the vendor has just turned up. If you don't mind waiting here, we'll see what's happening at the front.'

'We can wait.'

Harry and Queenie left the office.

'I tried to call you after the first new bid, but it went to your voicemail.'

'I saw that you'd tried to call and as I was busy at work and with talking to Queenie, I thought I'd call you back at lunchtime. Then when I got another call from Queenie to say there was another bid, I decided to come down and see if I could sort it out.'

'Nate suggested we do the same and look, here we are. Now there's a letter with another bid and the vendor's here. I wonder what's going to happen now?'

'I don't want to think about it, if this morning's any indication.'

I laughed. 'Indeed.'

It was almost thirty minutes before Harry returned.

'I'm not sure what to make of your expression,' I said as Harry sat down.

'Here's the short story,' began Harry. 'The vendor has

decided to auction.'

'What? We had first option, technically,' I insisted.

'I know, but it's the vendor's right,' explained Harry. 'He looked at what happened this morning, accepted the mix-up but then saw that someone else was interested and had offered $2.25 million.'

'We'll offer $2.4 million then,' I stated.

'You really want this building, don't you?'

'Yes, I do.'

'Okay, I'll put it to the vendor and let you know, but he seems pretty set on an auction now.'

'Do your best,' I said.

We left Harry's office and found somewhere to have some lunch.

'What if it does go to auction?' asked Alex.

'Then we bid until it's ours,' I responded.

'We'll need to talk about this.'

'I know we will, but not right now. Let's see if our offer is accepted first.

'I need to get back to work. I'll see you both tonight.'

Alex returned to work after the three of us shared an unexpected lunch. We discussed the morning's mix up and events, the new information about the vendor and his request for an auction. Nate and I then continued with the plans to do the grocery shopping, which needed to be done more regularly, and with a much fuller trolley, now that we had a teenager with hollow legs living with us.

19. Bids and Blobs.

I walked into the kitchen, the morning of the auction, not really knowing what I was doing. I can vaguely remember getting a mug from the cupboard for coffee, only to see one on the table for me. So I put it back. When I turned back to the table, Nate had started using it, so I went to the cupboard again. I sat at the table only to see an empty mug in front of me. Now I had two.

'What am I supposed to do with two mugs?' I asked, aimlessly.

Alex and Nate sniggered.

'Are you sure you're going to be all right this morning, sweetie? I can still take the day off,' offered Alex, taking the spare mug and putting it away.

'Let me be a nervous wreck on my own. Chrissy's coming with me, she'll keep me calm,' I replied. 'Anyway, you have that important business meeting to attend.'

'It can be put off for a few hours,' replied Alex.

'I think I'll be fine. Chrissy will keep me sane. I've given her permission to pinch, punch, poke or slap me if I get out of hand.'

Alex laughed. 'All the best and call me when it's over.'

'I will.' I kissed Alex as he left for work.

'Yeah, all the best,' echoed Nate.

'You get going to school,' I added.

Once I was alone, I had my shower and waited for Chrissy. She picked me up out the front of our house and we drove to the building. I dropped my stuff in my office at the Buckingham next door and went back outside. Harry arrived just as we emerged from the hotel.

'Hi, Harry.'

'Morning, Peter. You ready?' he responded.

'Probably not.' I laughed nervously.

'You'll be fine. Stick to your guns and budget and you won't be disappointed.'

'I'll try.'

We followed Harry to the first floor where it had been cleaned and prepared for the auction. Within half an hour, about a dozen people had arrived, along with the company's auctioneer. He called everyone's attention and ran over the details of the building and the procedures for the auction. He then began the bidding, opening at two million, three hundred thousand dollars.

'Do I hear 2.35?'

I nodded. We had begun

'2.35 million, with the gentleman on my left.'

'2.36,' came a bid from the opposite side of the room.

Was this the unknown bidder? I guess I'll never know.

'Do I hear 2.37?'

I nodded. I watched the man on the other side of the room; he waved his brochure at the auctioneer.

'2.38'

'2.4,' I called.

'2.45?' queried the auctioneer.

'2.5,' came a call from the back.

I turned around to see a suited man in dark glasses nodding to an unknown caller on his mobile phone. *Damn, this isn't going to be easy.*

'2.52?' queried the auctioneer.

I nodded.

‘2.53,’ called the second bidder.

‘2.55,’ came the call from the back.

The auctioneer looked at the man to his right. I was happy when his shook his head. He was out.

‘2.6,’ I called.

‘With you at the back?’ asked the auctioneer.

‘2.65,’ he replied.

‘Sir?’ the auctioneer looked at me.

‘2.7,’ I replied.

‘2.75,’ came the response from the back.

‘2.8,’ I said.

‘With you at the back.’

There was silence. I didn’t want to turn around.

‘If there are no more bids, the sale is going once …’

‘2.82,’ came the bid from the back.

The auctioneer looked at me. I looked at Chrissy for reassurance.

‘It’s your bid and it’s your place,’ she encouraged. ‘How much do you want it?’

I smiled at her resolutely and called in a strong voice, ‘2.85.’

‘Sir, it’s with you at the back of the room?’

Silence.

‘Going once.’

Silence.

‘Going twice.’

Silence.

‘If there are no more bids? Are we all done? … Sold for two million, eight hundred and fifty thousand dollars. Congratulations.’

Those gathered applauded.

For a moment I was stunned, and then came back to reality with a jolt when the most enthusiastic hug I’d received in a long time, attached itself to my neck.

‘Oh, sweetie, I’m so happy for you. Congratulations,’ said

Chrissy, exuberantly.

'I did it,' I exclaimed.

'Yes you did. Well done, Peter.' I turned to see Harry standing beside me.

'Thanks, Harry, for all your help and support.'

I turned to see the suited man pocket his mobile phone and leave the room and the other bidder from the beginning, come over.

'Well done. Congratulations,' he said.

'Thanks,' I replied.

'We just need to sign some paperwork, Peter,' interjected Harry.

'Sure,' I acknowledged. 'I'll be right back. Don't go away,' I said to Chrissy. 'Actually, I'll meet you back at the hotel.'

I followed Harry to a table and spent time signing the necessary paperwork to take ownership of the building, we had forty-five days to finalise the finance.

Thirty minutes later, I walked into the hotel.

'Break out the bubbly, my good man.'

'Already have. What are we celebrating this time?'

'Gather what staff we have, Vince.'

'Okay.' He left the bar.

I grabbed my mobile phone. 'Waiting, waiting,' I said and I thrummed my fingers on the bar. 'Hi sweetie. Hang on.'

Vince returned with the other two staff working that morning.

'Ah good, everyone's here. Alex, staff, it is with great delight that I inform you that just this hour, I signed the papers securing the purchase of the building next door.'

Vince almost dropped the bottle, thankfully saved it to continue pouring drinks. The other staff members were very happy.

'Congratulations, sweetie,' called Alex over the din.

'We're having a drink as we speak,' I replied, picking up

the phone. 'Don't worry, I'll bring some more home tonight.'

'How much did we pay for it?'

'$2.85,' I replied.

'A little more than we hoped, although less than what we said we would go to.'

'I'll tell you all about it tonight. Chat soon. Love you.' I took the drink Chrissy handed me.

* * * * *

There was no hesitation as to whom I'd use as the architect for the job.

'Can I speak to Mr Vaughan Long please?' I requested of the woman who answered my call.

'Who's calling please?' she queried.

'His brother, Peter Long-Smith.'

'One moment.'

'Thank you.'

'Petey, how's it going?'

'Doing well thanks, Vaguey.'

He laughed. 'It's hard being vague and an architect you now.'

'Oh, I'm sure you can still find a way.'

'Yeah, yeah. What do you want?'

'I want you to do some work for me?'

'I've told you before, you don't need an architect for a pergola. Unless you want some Romanesque styling?'

'You're funny.'

'Yes I am.'

'I've just bought a three storey building and I want to you to design the interior.'

'You did what?'

'You heard. Can I come over and talk to you about what I want?'

'Hang on.'

'Okay.' I heard him tapping away at his computer keyboard.

'Nope, it's not April 1.'

'Ha ha, that's tomorrow. Now, when can I come over?'

'Let me have a look.' Again, I heard tapping. 'You're in luck brother; I can see you first thing tomorrow.'

'Great, I'll see you at ten.'

'Ahem. I said first thing.'

'I heard. You start at ten, right?'

'Try eight.'

'Eight! How do you expect me to look my best at eight in the morning?'

'I'm sorry, I forgot you were a drama queen.'

'Only when the make-up goes on, thank you very much!'

Vaughan laughed. 'Well, you do a good show.'

'So you've finally seen one?'

'I told you I was coming that night.'

'I guess I forgot.'

'I've always heard the younger generation don't use their brains enough, so I guess your memory will go before mine.'

'Like hell it's gone.'

'Then I'll see you at eight?'

I sighed. 'I 'spose so.'

I walked into the lounge and plopped on the chair. The TV was on, but no one was watching it. Alex was reading the paper and Nate had a schoolbook open whilst stretched out on the floor.

'I'm seeing Vaughan tomorrow morning at eight.'

'How you gonna cope with that, sweetie,' replied Alex without looking up from the paper.

'Why is it that everyone thinks I'll have a problem being somewhere at eight?'

'Because you do. You always hated having to be at work at that time?'

'Pfft. Anyway, he said he'd have a look at my ideas.'

'So you've finished all the drawings and sketches?'

'No.'

'Then why are you sitting here chatting idly?'

'I love you too, honey.'

Nate sniggered.

'You down there, keep studying,' I teased.

*****

Two weeks after giving him the rough outline of what we wanted for the complex, I walked into his office. 'What have you got for me, Vaguey?'

'Hopefully something exciting,' he replied. He led me down the hall to a conference room.

Walking in, I saw several sketches lined up along one wall and I spotted several plans lying on the table. I looked over the sketches. 'Impressive ... interesting interpretations ... nice colours ... is that enough seating ... I thought the stage would be bigger.' I turned to where Vaughan stood. 'Tell me the story.'

We walked past each sketch in turn and Vaughan explained his interpretation of my vision and brief. I made mental notes of what I liked, further to what I had already expressed. I was determined to allow him to go through what he felt. We finally sat down and he went over the plans and their associated specifications.

'What do you think?' Vaughan asked, after his hour-long presentation.

'I think it's time for a drink,' I replied smiling.

Vaughan went over to the phone in the corner. 'Delores, can you bring in the morning tea please? Oh, can you also send in Adrienne and Marcus?'

'Right away Mr. Long.'

'I've asked them to join us,' he explained, noticing my confusion. 'They've been assisting me with this project.'

Delores knocked once and entered, pulling a trolley laden with cakes and tea and coffee. She set them up on a bureau at one end of the room.

'Thank you, Delores,' said Vaughan.

Delores nodded and exited. Vaughan directed me to the bureau and we helped ourselves to morning tea. As we sat down, Adrienne and Marcus entered carrying folios of papers.

'Peter Long-Smith, this is Adrienne Haywood and Marcus Patterson,' introduced Vaughan.

I shook their hands in turn.

'Peter, why don't you let us know what you think of the concepts and designs we've come up with?' said Vaughan.

'Firstly I want to say that I am very impressed and I'm looking forward to the final product,' I said. 'Having said that, there are some things I specifically want to discuss.'

Adrienne and Marcus looked a little concerned.

I smiled. 'Don't be worried, it's all good. Hasn't Vaughan prepared you for what I'm like?'

They nodded tentatively. I had to laugh. 'If you like, I can come back another day as my alter ego, then you'll know what hit you.'

'That won't be necessary, Peter.' Vaughan shot me a stern look.

'Then let's get to work,' I continued. 'Firstly, I want you to allow for changes on the ground floor. I want the existing café to be expanded by thirty percent into the middle vacant shop ...'

I continued to outline how I wanted the remaining ground floor space to house the main reception area at the front with a connecting door and passage into the Buckingham. A new staircase was to be installed against the far wall. Behind the reception area, the new cabaret room was to be built. The kitchen attached to the café was to be expanded sufficiently enough to service the café and cabaret room. I talked about how the showroom, on the first floor, was to have adequate space for both seated patrons there to enjoy a meal, or simply sit in the bar area and enjoy the shows. The stage was to be slightly larger than they had designed, but the space behind and around, could be reduced by the same amount. I indicated that I wanted some raised booths, as well as tables at floor level.

Once I'd signed the contracts at the end of March, I began negotiating with the owner of the café, to buy him out. It took lots of coffee and discussion, and then just before the end of April, the owner finally agreed to sell me the business. I reassured him that the current staff members were going to be retained, if they wanted, as I would still need them for the venture.

20. Plinka, Plinka, Parties, Pledges.

'Happy birthday Nate,' Alex and I said when Nate came down for dinner.

'Thanks,' replied Nate. He spied the gift and cards sitting on the table. 'Are they mine?'

'No. We thought we'd wrap a whole lot of things and give them away,' I replied sarcastically.

Nate looked at me warily.

'Of course they're yours,' I said. 'Happy birthday.'

I could see that Nate was getting teary.

'You don't have to open them now if you don't want to,' said Alex.

'As if,' replied Nate grabbing the first one.

'Sweeeet. An mp3 player,' responded Nate, a smile broadening his face. 'I've always wanted one of those.'

'Now you have one,' I said.

He opened one of the envelopes on the table.

'Wow, gift cards.' Nate was surprised.

'We thought this'd be easier than us trying to buy you clothes, etc.,' explained Alex. 'Unless you trust us of course?'

Nate smiled. 'I know you've seen what I wear and you'd probably do okay, but I appreciate the chance to go shopping myself. It's always been done for me.'

'We can do that on the weekend then,' I said.

'Sounds like a plan,' added Alex.

'We have one more for you,' I said, sliding another envelope across the table to him.

'More?' replied Nate. He opened the envelope quickly. Nate's eyes widened and he began to grin. 'Are you serious?'

'Yes we are,' I said. 'As you're now seventeen, you can come to one of my performances each week. As the rules also state, you are not to ask for anything alcoholic. Besides, the guys at the bar know better. They'll be told not to serve you anything other than soft drink.'

'Damn,' exclaimed Nate jovially.

* * * * *

Nate was ready as soon as dinner was finished the following Friday. He'd been to the hotel before, but for once, he didn't have to sit in the office doing homework waiting for Alex or me. He couldn't sit still the whole trip to the Buckingham. It was good to see him happy; particularly after how he was feeling the day he arrived.

The bar staff knew the rules and it was up to Vince to keep tabs on him. For the show itself, Nate sat with Alex and some of our friends.

I came on stage, wearing a tightly fitted jacket and a matching pleated short skirt supported by several layers of tulle, and danced and twirled around the floor, performing my rendition of the Bette Milder song, 'These Shoes'. I introduced The Poncettes and they belted out the tightly choreographed 'Three Little Maids' from The Mikado.

'Give it up for The Poncettes,' I chorused, walking back on stage. The crowd responded cheeringly. 'Now, a little birdie's told me that someone in the house tonight has had a birthday recently?' I looked down at Alex and nodded. I scanned the audience as well. 'Looks like we have more than one. Come up here boys, oh and a girl.'

Alex nudged Nate on stage. Joining him was another man and a stout woman.

'What brings you here tonight, darling?' I said, addressing the stout woman.

'My girlfriend dragged me here tonight,' she replied grumpily.

'Drag is the operative word here tonight, honey, and it's faaaabulous,' I directed to the audience. Various shouts and wolf whistles rang around the room. 'When's your birthday, honey?'

'Monday.'

'You stay right there and we'll have something for you later.'

'My husband is going to be alone tonight,' I said sidling up beside the tall dark-haired man standing on the stage. 'I hope you're single, my very handsome young friend?'

'No, I'm here with my wife,' he replied.

'Your wife!' I cried. 'No, no, no. You're too handsome to be straight.' The crowd laughed with me. 'Where is she?' He pointed to a very pretty redhead near the bar. 'You don't mind if I take him home tonight do you dear?'

She laughed and waved a hand in my direction. The husband looked mortified. 'Don't worry dear, I won't bite ... much.'

He began to look around nervously, trying to smile.

'Honey, it's all good. My bark is far worse than my bite,' I encouraged. 'When's your birthday?'

'It's today.'

'Happy birthday, sweetie.' I planted a huge red kiss on his cheek. I saw his wife laughing.

'Now, this is a first, a child on my stage,' I said to Nate. He was smiling and seemed to be revelling in the attention. 'Who do you belong to my sweet young thing?'

I could see Nate was about to indicate me but he quickly realised that was the wrong thing to do. 'That one there,' replied Nate, pointing to Alex.

'Alex, you're far too young to have a son this old,' I cooed.

'Oh no, he's not my dad, although he is my second dad,' said Nate quickly.

'He looks after you himself? I queried.

'No, I have two dads.'

'Lucky you.'

'Yes I am.' Nate smiled.

'Ah look, here come the cakes.'

Vince appeared through the crowd with three large cup cakes with bright pink icing and a lit candle on each. He gave one to each of those on stage.

'On the count of three ... one ... two ... three ... happy birthday to you ....' I began. After we'd finished singing, they blew out their candles. 'Make your way to the bar and Vince will fix you up with whatever you're having to drink.'

We then performed one of our fifteen-minute routines and that closed the first show.

* * * * *

It was easy to see that Nate had come home excited. Half the time he was talking so fast we couldn't understand him. When we did get him to slow down, he only sped up a few seconds later, so we just let him ramble on.

'Did you have a good time tonight, Nate?' asked Alex, as Nate placed another piece of his birthday cake in his mouth. Such moments of silence need to be utilised and quickly.

I think Nate mumbled something in reply about how much he enjoyed himself, but as his mouth was full, it was difficult.

'Finish your mouthful first, please,' I instructed.

I watched as Nate sat on a chair in the kitchen, then jumped up and tried to sit on the sink, only to get down and go look in the fridge.

I looked over at Alex. 'Too much sugar, methinks.'

'I agree.' Alex smiled. 'Now, Nate, let me ask again, did

you have a good time tonight?'

'Did I what? I'm used to hearing the music from the office. Not a fun thing, but seeing it live was so different and exciting. You're good, Dad.'

'Thanks.' I blushed.

'I want to get involved,' he said excitedly, before filling his mouth yet again.

'Get involved with what?' I asked.

'Performing,' Nate replied.

'I don't think so, Nate,' I replied.

'C'mon,' pleaded Nate.

'No,' stated Alex.

'Why not?' challenged Nate.

'You're too young,' I replied. 'You're also doing year twelve!'

'I'm not too young.'

'Yes you are, and you're also doing year twelve.'

'Fine then.' Nate stormed off.

'Leave him,' said Alex, as I went to follow. 'Sit down and have a cuppa. He'll be fine.'

*****

It was a week after Nate's birthday and we had all sat down for dinner.

'I'm glad it's Friday,' stated Alex.

'Busy week, hon?' I queried.

'Too many meetings. I'll be glad when this merger is done.'

'I have some news for you two,' announced Nate.

'Hope it's good,' I said.

'It's always good,' he replied.

'Like your first term report?'

'That's different.'

'Peter,' scolded Alex.

'Pffft,' said Nate, shrugging his shoulders. 'Moving right along ... I got a part in the school musical today.'

'You did?' I exclaimed. 'That's fantastic.'

'Yeah,' added Alex. 'What part did you get? What's the show?'

'Well, I didn't get the lead role, which I wanted, but I got the second lead,' explained Nate. 'My drama teacher also wants me to understudy the lead.'

'Congratulations. What's the show?'

'It's called Scamalot. It's a comedy.'

'Really? Sounds like fun,' I said. 'Are you the court jester, or something? You'd be good at that.'

'Get real. I'm no joker.'

'Ya could have fooled me.' I laughed.

'Whatever.'

'When's the show being presented?' asked Alex.

'We're doing it at the end of July,' replied Nate. 'Just after school goes back for term three. I think they're talking of having rehearsals over the school break.'

'That's a bit unfair, isn't it?'

'That's what we said. It's not confirmed. The teachers are hoping we'll do well before term ends.'

'Hang on a minute,' I said and interrupted the celebrations. 'How do you intend to fit rehearsal into your busy year twelve schedule?'

'I knew you were going to ask that, so I asked all my teachers for an update of my results,' he replied, calmly, almost smugly. 'Here,' he added, sliding an envelope across the table.

'All right, smarty, let's see.' I took the envelope and opened it. I watched Nate out of the corner of my eye. He continued to eat his dessert, but was smiling smugly as he did. 'I saw that.' I opened the piece of paper and was genuinely impressed. Since his first term results, he'd turned all his marks around and was travelling in the top ten percent of his class. 'I'm impressed.'

'So I can be in the school play?' he asked eagerly.

'If your results slip, you will withdraw. Deal?'

'Deal.'

*****

April that year was a nightmare. There were endless parades to various council agencies and state government bodies. Thankfully, Aidan, now employed as my production assistant and booking manager, was a great benefit. With his theatre industry contacts, he calmly went about business and never complained once. Well, not to me anyway. Although we already had licences relating to the Buckingham, because we were expanding into food, we had to update them. I had to go to council to confirm the permits and agreements for the alterations we wanted to make. I made yet another trip to see Vaughan regarding the plans and get them submitted to council. After all that, I needed another holiday.

I'd had enough for one day and I came home from work early. There are only so many times you can look at colours and wood and paint and fittings. With my mind all over the place, I slumped into the lounge in the front room, popped off my shoes and plonked my legs over the arm. I grabbed a cushion and covered my face with it. Don't panic, I wasn't about to kill myself, I just wanted silence from all the noise of the construction.

However, my struggle for silence was being assaulted by an unusual sound. I was too exhausted to get up, so I lay there listening to it. The more I listened, the more familiar the sound became. I sat up, tossed the pillow aside and listened intently this time. 'It sounds like a pi......'

I realised what was happening. I sat down quietly and listened. It had to be Nate tinkling away on the old piano.

Oh my, it's so out of tune it's not funny. I must get on to that for Nate. I sat there and absorbed the out of tune sounds coming from the back of the house.

After a while it stopped. I heard movement, so I thought I'd better make some noise. I quietly got up, opened the front door and then closed it very loudly.

'You home, Nate?' I called, as I picked up my backpack

and threw it on to the couch.

'Yeah, in the kitchen,' he replied.

'Leave something for me.'

'I always do.' I heard him chuckling.

'Yeah right,' I said, entering the kitchen. 'Hey, did I hear the piano going just now, when I came in?'

'No,' Nate replied quickly, although a little sheepishly. 'It'd be out of tune, surely. It looks old enough.'

'Perhaps I should get it tuned anyway.'

'Meh.' Nate left quickly, a plate piled high with food.

'I hope you're going to eat your dinner tonight,' I commented to his retreating back, but got no reply.

I got the piano fixed, however I never heard it being played until months later. At the time, I reckon Nate only played it until he knew we'd be home.

* * * * *

'I'm impressed,' I said, after we'd attended Nate's school production at the beginning of third term. 'Nate, you're a natural.'

'I thought so too,' agreed Alex.

'Thanks,' replied Nate from the back seat of the car. 'Does that mean I can join your show?'

'I must admit, I have been thinking.'

'No,' stated Alex firmly.

Nate and I were quiet for the remainder of the trip home. Nate took his things upstairs and headed for a shower. Alex and I hung around in the kitchen.

'Why not,' I said.

'He's too young, and he has to study,' replied Alex.

'No he's not! Besides, his school work is more than up to scratch.'

'Yes ... he ... is!' Alex raised his voice slightly.

'No, he is not!' I replied raising my voice to his level. 'He's talented, can sing and is a bloody good dancer and actor.'

'He should be concentrating on school, not worrying about performing on a regular basis.'

'Oh, so now it's a worry to perform regularly.' I was furious.

'That's not what I meant.'

'It certainly sounded like it.' I stormed from the kitchen. I wasn't looking where I was going and I crashed heavily into Nate, sending him sprawling across the dining room floor.

'I'm sorry, Nate,' I apologised and helped him to stand. 'Are you okay?'

'Yeah. Are you okay though?'

'I'm fine,' I replied gruffly.

'It didn't sound like it.'

I stopped suddenly and faced him. 'You heard us?'

'I think the whole street did.'

'Oh.' I looked up and saw Alex standing in the kitchen doorway.

'I'm still interested in performing. That's why I did this school play. I like performing, but I'm not into drag.'

'That's okay, Nate. I'd love to have you in the show.'

'He's not doing it!' Alex stated.

Nate looked back and forth between Alex and me.

'I think for now, we don't discuss this anymore tonight or for the rest of the weekend. We all need time to calm down and think more rationally.'

'Agreed,' said Alex.

* * * * *

It was another week before Alex and I sat and talked about Nate and the disagreement we'd had over his performing.

'Now that Nate's out of the house, we can talk about last weekend,' I said at lunch on Saturday. 'I know I haven't changed my mind.'

'Neither have I.'

'So we're still at first base. Let's talk about the pros and cons. We both have to try and keep an open mind and listen to each other?' I suggested.

'I can handle that. Who's first?'

'I do want to apologize for being such a shithead last weekend,' I continued. Alex smiled. 'I'm not going to make excuses either. I firmly believe that Nate is old enough to perform in the show with me and be able to maintain his studies.'

'I think that with all he's been through, he needs to settle down and have some normality and stability,' Alex countered.

'He knew what he was doing when he chose to come looking for me. Keeping him strictly to school is unwise as well. It doesn't look like he's into sport, and I don't want him sitting behind a computer either.'

'Agreed.' Alex paused. 'I just think he's too young to know what he wants to do.'

'Why do you say that? Because of his family history?'

'No!' Alex was indignant. 'That's not what I meant.'

'Then what did you mean?'

'I simply meant that because he's been through so much change, he should concentrate on something regular and stable.'

'From the reports we've seen, I don't think he's ever had a problem with school work, despite that glitch in first term when he was settling in.'

Alex stroked his chin.

'What else is going on in your mind sweetie? What aren't you talking to me about? What are you holding back?'

'I've been thinking about leaving work as well.'

'Oh. When did you start down this track?'

'When we bought the building next to the Buckingham.'

'So why all this shit about Nate?'

'I'm feeling left out,' replied Alex.

'Oh, sweetie,' I said, moving around the table to hug him. 'Don't be like that. Why do you feel left out?'

''Cause you get to spend more time with Nate than I do and if he starts performing, I'll hardly have anytime with him.'

'Honey, I'd never leave you out of anything to do with Nate. I love you, very much.'

'I know. It's just the way I'm feeling.'

'Then why don't you leave work? One of us can run the Buckingham, the other the new venue and we'll both be around for Nate.'

'That'd work.'

'Here's another idea,' I added. 'What about you be home for Nate after school and stuff and I'll have him with rehearsals and performing. That way we're both spending time with him. Perhaps we can take it in turns to spend one day a month with him. A special time with one of us and Nate.'

Alex smiled broadly and wiped tears from his eyes. 'You know, that just might work.'

'So you'll let Nate be in the show?'

'I'd want to work out some pretty strong guidelines for all of us abide by.'

'I can work with that.'

* * * * *

Nate was home for dinner that same night and we passed on the good news.

'Alex and I had another chat today,' I informed Nate.

'Do I need to check with the neighbours about what was said?'

'Cheeky bugger,' I countered. 'No you don't. We were quite civilised.'

'We have good news for you,' said Alex.

'I can perform?' Nate asked, a hint of excitement in his voice.

'Yes you can,' informed Alex.

'Woo hoo.' Nate punched the air with his fist.

'However,' interrupted Alex.

'I knew it couldn't last,' said a mockingly dejected Nate.

'There are some guidelines we've worked out.'

'Let's get it over with then,' said Nate.

'Here's the deal,' I said. 'School is always first, especially exams. You can perform twice a month at the new venue in the early shows. If your school results begin to falter, or drop below an acceptable standard, your performances will be restricted or cancelled. You will rehearse once a week with the troupe, which will be right after school.'

'As we said, these are guidelines and they apply to us all,' added Alex. 'It doesn't mean you can be blasé about any of them either. We will enforce them if we have to and you have to abide by them. That okay with you, Nate?'

'I think I can handle that,' agreed Nate. 'I'll make the promise that I will try my best.'

'That's all we ask,' said Alex. 'Oh, and I have another piece of news for you?'

'What's that?' said Nate.

'I'm going to leave work,' said Alex. 'That way, we can concentrate on you and our business without having to worry about working for anyone else.'

'Does that mean I'll have to go to the Buckingham every night after school?' asked Nate.

'Not at all. You know you're allowed to be here at home after school on your own sometimes,' said Alex. 'Although we are planning to make sure one of us is at home when you get out of school ...'

'... Except the night you rehearse,' I added.

'Fair enough.'

'To exciting times,' I said, raising my glass.

'To exciting times,' echoed Alex and Nate.

'One more thing, Nate,' added Alex. 'I think it'd be good if you started taking piano lessons. Make the gift you've got better.'

'How did you know I played piano?' he queried, looking furtively from Alex to me.

'A little birdie told me one day that they heard you playing an out of tune piano,' Alex explained. 'Then, when said piano had been fixed, it was never heard again.'

'Who heard me play?' he was a little indignant and embarrassed.

'I did,' I replied sheepishly. 'That one day, weeks ago when I heard you play the out of tune thing in the back room, to which you denied having played.'

Nate now looked sheepish.

'Anyway, I had it tuned and I never heard it again,' I continued. 'I figured you'd either stopped playing or made sure you'd finished before either of us got home.'

'I did sort of try and work out when to stop,' said Nate. 'I don't play that often, even though I knew it had been tuned.'

'Now you have no excuse,' encouraged Alex. 'If you want, we'll have the back room soundproofed so you can play to your heart's content and not disturb anyone.'

'Do I still have to take lessons?' Nate asked.

'We'd like you to,' replied Alex.

'I guess that'll be okay. Could it wait until after exams?'

'That might be a good idea. We don't want you stressing over having to do too much, now that you're performing,' I agreed.

21. Additions and Arrivals.

The work on the new venue was finished by the end of July. Thankfully, it was on schedule. Now that Alex had left work, we sat down and worked out who'd be doing what. We decided Alex would look after the business management of the two venues, with help from Vince, whilst I'd look after the entertainment, with help from Aidan.

'When do you want to plan the opening sweetie?' I asked Alex when we knew the work was nearly finished.

He pulled his laptop off the coffee table and opened up a program. 'Well, looking at the spreadsheet we drew up a few months ago, Friday August 15 is looking the best.'

I leaned over and had a look. 'Yeah, that should work. That gives us about three weeks to advertise.'

'Is everything ready?'

'The boys have been helping and Aidan has been a gem. All he's waiting on is the date.' I straightened up on the couch. 'I'll tell him tomorrow.'

'Are we still happy with the name's we've chosen?'

'It's a bit late to change now,' I stated gruffly. 'The signage was ordered weeks ago.'

'Calm down, sweetie, I was only asking.'

'Well, we're calling the venue itself *Bucky's*,' I said.

'I think that's still a good choice,' replied Alex.

'It's cute. We're calling the cabaret room, *The Nedelina Room.*'

'That was a good idea of yours to honour Aunt Nedelina.'

'We owe her quite a lot. I just wish she was here to see all this.'

'She gave us quite a lot. She'll be watching,' said Alex. 'What are we calling the showroom again?'

'*The Lincoln Room*?'

'I did like that one.'

'That was my choice too,' I agreed.

'At least that's settled.'

* * * * *

Despite the finalised decisions about the building and signage, the troupe was another thing. I'd spent the morning making calls and confirming deliveries of various items for the new venue.

Just after lunch, I was startled by a knock on the door.

'Come in,' I called.

'Hi, Peter, I'm Perry Li,' he greeted, holding out his hand.

I looked up to see Perry Li poking his head through the door. I'd never met him in person, though I did know his alter ego, Gyna Cologist.

Perry stood at 170cm tall, had jet black hair, dark eyes and fine features. He's fit but I was surprised at how strong he was when we shook hands. Very firm. I smiled to myself. It was refreshing to receive such a greeting from a gay man. You get so sick of the limp fish handshake very quickly.

'Have a seat,' I said, offering him one of the couches I had in the office, as I sat on the other one. 'How can I help you today, Perry?'

I could see him hesitating.

'Uhm.' He took a deep breath. 'I was wondering if you needed an extra performer?'

He caught me completely off guard. I tried to be coy about it. 'What makes you think I perform?'

He smiled. 'I kinda found out who you are.'

'Really? What did you find out?'

'Who you perform as.'

'Who would that be?'

'Prissy DuPonce.'

'I see. How did you find that out?'

'By accident really.'

'Oh?' I was curious and looked at Perry a little more intently.

'I was at the Buckingham one night and being late, my friends and I were only able to find space in the back room. I saw a couple of the performers come down stairs and quickly move backstage. The last to descend was Prissy. Just before she vanished backstage, I saw her give a very personal greeting to another man. I found out that it was Alex Long-Smith, one of the owners and that he owned the venue with his partner.'

'Me.'

'Yes, you. So I worked out you were Prissy DuPonce. I started smiling like a Cheshire cat and my friends grilled me mercilessly about it, but I didn't say a word.'

'Thanks for that.'

'Anyway, over the past couple of months, I've been finding it difficult to maintain my performance levels where I am at the moment.'

'Whom are you performing with at present?' I queried.

'Freda Mingle.'

'I see. What's the problem then?'

'I just feel I can be a better performer if I was away from Freda.'

'Well, I hadn't thought of putting on someone else, however I will speak with the troupe.'

'I'd appreciate it.'

I showed Perry out and wandered back through the bar to

my office.

That night I shared with the others about my visit from Perry and after a lot of convincing from them, I agreed to take Perry on, giving us another performer. I rang Perry the next day, offered him a position, and had him start that week. After all, it was now less than three weeks to opening. He needed the time to become familiar with the routines. Thankfully, he picked them up quickly and fitted in very well.

*****

Why is it that on the days of big events, I can't sleep in. I mean, I was in the kitchen at seven a.m. cooking breakfast. What gives?

By seven-thirty, Alex and Nate were also enjoying the very big breakfast I'd cooked.

'Did you have to make so much noise?' complained Nate, shovelling yet another forkful of scrambled eggs into his mouth.

'Like you slept well last night,' I replied. 'I heard you going back and forth to the bathroom. I should be complaining about you keeping me awake.'

Nate laughed.

'I should be having a go at the both of you then,' chimed in Alex.

'What's the matter, hon,' I cooed jokingly. 'You miss your ugly sleep too?'

'Bite me. You tossed and turned all night long. I was tempted to come downstairs and sleep in the spare bed.'

'You couldn't 'coz you knew I was in it,' came an elderly female voice.

'Morning, Mum.' I got out of my seat and greeted my mother with a kiss.

'Morning, dear,' added Alex.

'Morning, Gran,' said Nate, smiling.

'You can call me, Evelyn, Nate, I really don't mind,' she

said.

'I know that,' replied Nate. 'I've never had a real gran and I kinda like calling you that. Mum's mum died when I was young and I was never introduced to my stepfather's parents.'

'As long as you're comfortable.' Evelyn gave Alex a kiss on the head and Nate a hug. 'Did you make any coffee?'

'Not long brewed, Mum. How do you want it today?'

'Black, with a little bit of milk.'

I looked at Mum and rolled my eyes. Nate grinned.

'Where do you intend to put all of that, young man?' stated Evelyn spying Nate's extremely large plate of food.

'He'll eat that much again at lunchtime,' I said. 'I wish I had his metabolism.'

We laughed and chatted and by nine, the kitchen was as clean as it was before I started.

We'd allowed Nate to stay home from school the day Bucky's opened. He'd be too excited to concentrate on anything anyway. Knowing Nate, he'd want to help where he could.

We piled into the car and headed for Bucky's. Pulling into our reserved car park at the back of the building, a sense of apprehension rose in me. I'd been to the venue every day that week, except now I was about to show my mother. A woman who'd overseen the interior decorating needs of the well to do in all the state capitals for nearly fifteen years now. *What would she say? How would she react? Would she like the décor? The arrangements? The colours?*

'What's the matter, Peter?' she asked as I unlocked the back door to the Buckingham.

'Nothing, I'll be fine.'

'No you're not. You're worried about something. You can tell your mother.'

'It's nothing.'

'He's nervous about your reaction,' said Alex, smirking slightly. I'd told Alex not to mention my concerns to my mother, but no, he had to tell.

'Gee, thanks, sweetie.'

'I'm glad you told me, Alex. It would've bothered me all day otherwise.' Evelyn hooked her arm around Alex's and strolled inside. Nate and I brought up the rear. 'So. What's this place look like then?'

We put our stuff in the office and we walked towards the new doorway.

'I see you've linked the hotel to the rest?' she noted.

'Yes. That way people who want to stay on after a show can do it in the Buckingham whilst the rest of the venue is closed,' I explained.

Walking into the foyer area, Mum was looking up, down and all around. I listened to the occasional 'hmm' and 'interesting'.

'What's interesting?' I asked nervously.

'Nothing dear. This foyer is very nice indeed,' she replied. 'I like the way you've used the gold mesh curtains on the windows.'

'We had talked about painting over them, but by restricting the amount of daylight and streetlight we let in, we created a sense of intrigue inside.'

'Very wise, Petey.' Evelyn let go of Alex and walked into the Nedelina Cabaret Room.

'That part was Vaguey's ... I mean Vaughan's idea.'

'You didn't say Vaughan helped you here?'

'Yes I did, many times. Besides, I'm sure Vaughan told you as well.'

'He might've mentioned something.'

Standing at the back of the room, Evelyn looked around. I went over to a panel behind the bar and turned on the house lights. After a few minutes, I turned off the house lights and turned on the lighting that would be used for the room itself. The room was bathed in a soft, warm glow.

'Wow.'

'I gather you like it, Mum?'

'I do indeed.'

Walking past the front desk, Mum ran her hand along the black wall housing the sound and light desks. She moved past that and into the main room.

'Tiered. Smart'

Mum moved in further. She stepped up to one of the semi-circular booths and sat down. Her hands smoothed over the black leather covered seats and dark polished wooden tables. I held Alex's hand and waited patiently. I saw her looking over to the similar booths on the opposite wall.

She stepped down and inspected the range of tables placed on the floor between the sets of booths. She walked back towards where we were and stood at the bar. She walked its length, dragging her hand behind her.

'I'm glad you matched the material for the bar top and tables.'

'I tried. What do you think of ....'

Mum held up her hand. 'Uh!' she said short and sharp.

Mum continued to walk around the room. She gazed at the walls and the accoutrements. She stepped onto the stage and looked back to the bar, where we'd moved.

'Is she always like this?' asked Nate quietly.

'Yes,' I replied. 'Especially when dealing with décor.' Nate nodded.

Watching Mum, I still liked how the stage looked. At first, I wanted to have it big enough to hold a baby grand piano. Alex talked me out of it saying it would've been too big. I certainly didn't want to make the backstage areas too small for the artists. It kept me awake for a few nights until I hit upon an idea;

I'd been walking through the new building, checking to see how the works were going. As I perused the top floor, where our rehearsal rooms would be, I realised the amount of space we actually had to use. I ran down to look at the plans for both the cabaret and showrooms. That night at dinner, Alex noticed the twinkle I had in my eye.

'Okay, what happened to you today?' he asked.

'I think I may have resolved the stage issue for the cabaret room,' I said to Alex at dinner.

'I thought we'd decided on that already?' replied Alex.

'So did I,' added Nate.

'I was happy with what had been decided, at that stage ...' I continued. I watched Alex rub his brow. 'Anyways, I was thinking that we can make the rooms behind the stage a bit smaller by having all the changing rooms on the second floor. Yes, yes, I know it's a long way to travel, but we have the space up there to do it. Then we make sure the space backstage is comfortable enough for when they're waiting. Instead of a five minute call, we give them a fifteen minute call.'

'Hmmm.' Absent-mindedly, Alex rested his pasta covered fork on his lower lip.

'Ahem,' I interrupted. 'You now have a nice smear of sauce running down your hand.'

'Ooops.' He wiped away the mess. 'I like the idea. I think we can make that work.'

Now, tucked away in the far corner of the stage, was the smallest black baby grand piano we could find. It snuggled up against the burgundy drapes we used to frame the stage.

With a clap of her hands, Mum stepped off the stage and walked lightly to where I was. She threw her arms around my neck and kissed me. 'You've made me proud, Peter.'

'Thanks, Mum.'

'I particularly like the way you've used back lighting on the lighter wooden panels along the walls. They give enough light for people to see what they're doing. Coupled with the burgundy, cream and pale blue wallpaper, the ambience is nicely set. What's this room going to be used for?'

'I wanted it to be a little different. This is the Nedelina Room. Somewhere that's intimate for meals as well as being close to really enjoy the entertainment.'

'That's a nice touch, Peter. You've done well. Although it does remind me of something I've seen in certain books,' she added, throwing me a wry smile.

'I wanted the best. So I consulted the best.'

'Looks like Vaughan did too. I knew I raised good boys.'

'Shall we have a look at the next level?' said Alex. 'Or would you like a coffee?'

'Let's look upstairs first,' said Evelyn enthusiastically.

We walked up the newly installed grand old Gullywood-style staircase and I unlocked the showroom doors. Thinking back, I can't remember if Alex had seen the finished Lincoln Room or not, but it was evident that Nate hadn't.

'Holy shit!'

'Nate. Language, please,' I said.

'Leave him alone, Peter,' Mum said. 'Would you rather I say it?' I looked at her and she smiled. 'Let's go have a look.' Mum stepped into the foyer area and led the way. Moving past the greeting area, mum walked beside the curved bar.

I felt it safe to let Mum wander about on her own. Alex and I sat down in one of the closer booths whilst Nate jumped up and sat on the bar.

'Don't let Vince catch you doing that,' I said, mockingly waving a finger at him.

'I'll just tell him you let me.'

'Oh really?'

'Yes.'

'Shoosh, you two,' called Mum from the other end of the raised booths. 'What's the black one in the corner dear?'

'Sound and lights, Mother dearest,' I answered. 'Like the one downstairs.'

'Ah.' She sat down in a booth in front of it. 'I'm glad to see you get a good view of the stage this far back.'

'I didn't want anyone to miss out,' I called, not moving from my position.

'Peter dearest, sit with me.'

'Now you're in for it,' said Nate.

'Keep that up and you will be too,' I responded. Nate shrugged his shoulders and grinned.

I walked along beside the raised booths and sat down next to mum.

'Navy and purple? Not something I'd do, but it seems to work.'

'It took a while to find the colour mix of the purple and the navy, and then I thought it needed cheering up.'

'I've not heard it referred to as 'cheering up' before.'

'So you do like the accents of aqua and white?'

The row of raised booths was across the back and down one side. The tables and chairs on the remaining floor space. A small band area completed the size of the curved stage. Navy and purple dominated the colour scheme on the walls and the surrounds of the booths, with the accents of aqua and white lifting the room. The wall and table lights were art deco in basic design, but had a modern interpretation that added to the style, romance and ambience of the room. It looked glamorous.

'I daresay that if I tried this in some of the dowager's homes I'd normally decorate, I'd lose a modicum of reputation.'

I laughed, saw Alex pop his head up and Nate look in our direction. I watched Alex get up and go behind the bar as we'd stocked one of the fridges with a good supply of champagne and he held up one of the bottles, showing three fingers on the other hand. I nodded and showed him four fingers. Alex nodded in Nate's direction and I smiled. Alex retrieved four glasses and popped the cork.

'I don't need to walk around as much as I did downstairs, I can see all that I need to from here,' Mum said.

'Okay then,' I replied.

'What's behind the back wall?'

'From left to right, there are the toilets, backstage, the kitchen and a walkway to the change rooms on the next level up. Let's go to the bar, Mum, I think Alex has the champagne ready.' I took Mum by the arm and we walked down the stairs and crossed the floor amidst the tables to the bar.

'So, Evelyn, did he throw a prissy-fit?'

'What did you say?' I declared, looking at him.

'Just making sure you weren't reacting like you did after your work function last year.'

'How did you find out about that?'

'The boys told me.'

'I'll have to have words with them.'

'Evelyn, did he do a prissy?'

'Well, what did he do after the staff function?'

'Nothing,' I replied, crossing my arms across my chest.

'I wasn't talking to you, sweetie,' Evelyn answered. 'What did he do, Alex?'

'Basically, he began flapping about when his work colleagues wanted pictures of him as Prissy,' he explained.

'Is that all?'

Nate sniggered and Alex gave me a hug. 'It's all in good fun, hon. When the boys told me, it was funny.'

'So, now whenever I have a little bit of an issue with something …'

'… you'll be going all prissy.'

'Nice,' I said sarcastically.

'Here, drink this.' Alex handed us a drink. 'Here's to Bucky's.'

'To Bucky's.' we echoed.

22. Beginnings.

It was now six in the evening. The boys and I had rehearsed all afternoon and there wasn't a whole lot more we could do.

Zachary Thumm had arrived and everything was set up for him. Zachary is a young, gay comedian and singer. He's performed at a few places around town, particularly during MydSumma, the annual gay and lesbian festival of culture, arts and community. I remembered hearing an interview with him on Melvegas' gay radio station, JAY FM, and thought he'd be a good addition to our program. I mentioned it to Aidan, who duly made the booking. We'd booked him for the Nedelina Cabaret Room for two weeks. On opening night, he was obviously as nervous as we all were. I'd seen a part of his rehearsal earlier in the evening and was wishing I could be there to see it. Thankfully, Alex was going to be the master of ceremonies for the two rooms for the evening.

Yes, I can hear every one of you thinking, since when did Alex become superman? Well, he didn't (but always has been in my eyes). Anyway, Alex was going to be able to host both rooms because we had staggered start times between the two rooms.

I was upstairs in our changing rooms when mum and Nate arrived. 'You're here early.'

'It was either be nuisances here or be stir crazy at home,'

said Mum.

'What did she do to you, Nate?'

'Nothing, Dad,' he replied. 'I think we did it to each other really.' He smiled.

'Oh?' I looked at my mother.

'After we went home with Alex to let you rehearse, we had lunch and did the housework ...'

'... Why did you let Gran do the housework?' I said turning to Nate.

'Alex tried to stop her, but she insisted, so he let her help. In fact, we *all* did the housework.'

'Nate, you never do the housework.'

'There's always a first. Besides, Gran kept hassling me.'

'Mum!'

'Calm down, sweetie. A boy needs to learn how to look after his home. Teaching you never did you any harm. Think only of tonight,' Mum replied.

'Then because we'd finished it so early, we had nothing to do for the rest of the afternoon,' added Nate.

'Alex had some last minute shopping to do for tonight, so that left Nate and me to try to entertain ourselves,' explained Mum.

'I see.'

'Alex came home, we had an early dinner ...,' explained Mum.

'... More like a big, late afternoon tea ...,' added Nate.

I laughed.

'... then we came down here. Alex is in the building somewhere, hassling some poor staff member for having his shirt untucked no doubt.'

'I was not, thank you very much, Evelyn!' stated Alex as he walked in the door, Zachary following him. 'How you doing, sweetie?' he added coming over to me and giving me a kiss.

'I'll tell you after I've had a bottle of champagne.'

'Well, you're not having a whole bottle, nevertheless I did

bring up one for us *all* to share. Gather round folks.'

Mum, Nate, Zach and the troupe gathered around Alex and me. We all took a glass from the table. 'Here's to strength, good memories, relaxation, fun and a successful thrust into the entertainment industry here in Melvegas.'

After the toast, I went for a walk around the entire venue. Coming down to the first floor, I walked along the access hall leading to the stage. I popped into the kitchen and everything seemed to be moving along well.

'That's not what I told you to do,' the head chef barked to a junior.

I nodded at Gerard, backed out of the kitchen feeling confident that all was going well in there and walked backstage.

I spotted Roy, our props manager. 'How's it going, Roy?'

'All connected and working properly. I don't anticipate any problems,' he replied.

'It's comforting to have someone on board who knows what they're doing.'

'Thanks for the chance. I must admit, when I first saw the job ad, I wasn't so sure. After talking to you and hearing your enthusiasm and realising it was the same Prissy DuPonce who'd be running the show, I decided to apply.'

'As far as Alex and I are concerned, you were the best we saw. We even had people applying with no technical experience at all.'

'Now that would've been fun.'

'At least we're not finding out now,' I replied. 'Remember to relax.'

'Shouldn't that be my line to you?' encouraged Roy.

'I have a fantastic team, I'm sure everything will be okay.'

I moved through the wings, stepped onto the stage, and was blinded by a spotlight. 'What the …' I called.

'Get uzed to it.' A heavily accented reply came out of the darkness.

'I hope it's not going to be that bright tonight, Tyco?'

'Not all ze time,' he replied, laughing. 'I don't zink ve'll ever need it zis bright. I couldn't pass up ze opportunity.'

'I must remember to review all contracts immediately.'

Tyco's infectious laughter echoed throughout the empty showroom. Stepping off the stage, he dimmed the spotlight. I walked amongst the tables and stepped up to one of the booths just below the Tech booth. 'How's it looking for tonight, Tyco?'

'You dezigned ze lighting Pe-ter, I've just put it all togezer. Have a look,' he said, nodding his head towards the stage.

'Wow, that looks great,' I said, enthusiastically.

'Zank you, Pe-ter,' replied Tyco.

What I hadn't noticed when I first stepped onto the stage, was the flurry with which the waiters were scurrying about the showroom. 'It's the other way around,' berated one to another. 'I've already told you,' he added tensely.

'Dante, what's up?' I called.

'Hi, Peter,' he replied, rushed. 'Just making sure everything is right.' He turned towards the bar, raised his hand and was about to say something.

'I wouldn't do that if I were you,' I urged. 'Vince knows what he's doing.'

'It looks all wrong…'

'Be warned then.'

I turned and watched as the stage was bathed in all manner of colour. Spots came and went on various points around the stage. The curtains closed and then opened again. Theatrical smoke filtered along the floor in a brief burst. For some extremely odd reason, I even had a bubble machine installed, which was now filling the air with bubbles.

'What was I thinking?' I muttered more to myself than Tyco.

A hearty laugh filled the showroom. 'It'z all about fun, Madame DuPonce.'

I turned suddenly at the sound of crashing glass.

'Everyone okay?' I called to the bar, where I saw a barely

controlled Vince standing, his hands firmly holding the edge of the bar, glaring at an even more flustered Dante.

I moved down to the floor and walked over to the bar. 'Dante, walk with me a moment.' Dante followed me a few paces away from the bar and a seething Vince. 'Did I not warn you about that?'

'It needed to be fixed,' Dante pleaded.

'From memory, Vince is bar and you are floor service?'

Dante took a moment to reply.

'Humour me and answer the question.'

'That's correct.'

'Good. Now go and do that.' I moved away from Dante. 'Vince, you okay here?'

'I will be,' he replied.

'That's what I like to hear. Talk to me later, won't you.'

'Sure thing, *Boss*.'

Anyone with half a brain couldn't miss the emphasis Vince placed on the word 'boss' and it was loud enough for all to hear.

Vince was by far the best asset we had. I had no qualms about him leaving the bar at the Buckingham to run the showroom. Not long after we'd started, we'd placed him in control of the entire bar staff with strict instructions to make sure he moulded as many of the staff after himself. He was the best and I know there had been occasions when others had tried to poach him away. He's now a guest lecturer at the best known hospitality course in town.

I left the showroom and walked down the wide staircase to the ground floor. As I entered the main foyer, I looked into the bar at the Buckingham and saw quite a few people enjoying a drink. I turned and began walking to the Nedelina Cabaret Room.

'Looking good here, Miranda?' I said as I approached the woman standing behind the service desk.

'Thankfully, all staff members have reported in.'

'You sure all staff have reported in?'

'Why, what's happened?' she said urgently.

'Nothing really,' I replied calmly. 'I just saw Dante seemingly running things upstairs.'

'Oh yeah, Andrew called in sick,' she admitted. 'I've known that he'd probably not be here tonight, he was so sick on Monday and that he's been resting all week. He sounded worse today when he rang me, so I had to make a last minute change.'

'You might want to debrief the showroom staff afterwards. I'm not sure if Dante is the best for that role.'

'Sorry, Peter,' apologised Miranda.

'I'm not blaming you at all, Mir, it's been a tense week.'

'I'll get it sorted.'

'I know you will. Any other news?'

'The café is doing well,' she responded, nodding in the café's direction. 'The line outside is starting to grow and at last check, we were actually booked out for tonight and tomorrow night.'

'Wow, I hadn't heard,' I said excitedly. 'You've got the table saved in both rooms for Mum, Nate and our invited guests?'

'Yes we have, Peter. They can move between rooms as they please.'

'Thanks, Mir,' I said, kissing her on the cheek. 'Have Alex or I mentioned that people have to book for each room separately?'

'Yes, Peter, many, many times.'

'Oh.'

'It's fine though,' she said with a smile. 'No, Dave, the doors open at seven. They'll just have to wait,' she added addressing the staff member who'd just interrupted her. 'Sorry about that.'

'I'll let you get back to work,' I said.

'Have a fantastic show.'

'I'll try. Make sure the staff know that the back room in the Buckingham has been set aside for the function and will be open from about nine-thirty onwards.'

'I will. Now go. I'm about to open the doors.'

'Yes, go, before I have you escorted away,' came the voice from behind me.

'Alex,' I said, turning to face him. He stood there, looking like he stepped off a movie set. He was wearing three-quarter length jacket and black pants, white shirt and jade green vest. 'You look stunning.'

'Thanks, Sweetie,' he replied. 'As for you, you have an hour and half to become stunning. You'd better get started.'

'Normally I'd make a comment right about now ...'

'... yeah, yeah, yeah ...'

'... but I'm going to take your advice and vanish upstairs and get ready.'

'Good boy.'

23. Boogie Woogie, Sparkles and Song.

When Alex walked into the change rooms at seven forty-five, I was thankful he had more champagne with him. 'I hope we have enough left for later.'

'Yes, dear. Don't worry your pretty red head about it.' The others laughed. 'To tonight,' Alex toasted.

'To tonight,' we echoed.'

I sculled my champagne like it was water. 'I needed that.' Everyone looked at me; their glasses still at least three-quarters full. 'Well I did. If any of you want to take over, then be my guest.' I stepped out of my shoes and pushed them to the middle of the room.

There was a long silence. Then it started. Rory began to snigger, grabbing one of the Chinese fans to cover his face. Then Aidan joined in. Soon Mick, Alex and Dean started. Finally, Perry and I began. We laughed so hard we cried. I managed to stop as I had to attend to my make-up, as did the others.

'After that, I reckon I could take on Everest in these shoes.' The laughter started again. 'Enough already!'

'Let's go, Aidan. I'm sure we should be doing stuff downstairs,' announced Alex, holding the door open. 'See you after the shows.'

After Alex and Aidan had left, we went back to adding

the finishing touches. I took a moment to scan the faces of my troupe.

'What's the matter, Perry?' I asked, sitting beside him.

'Technically, this is my first performance with you girls.'

'Technically, yes. It's not your first time on a stage, though.'

'No. I'm glad to be away from, Freda. We weren't seeing eye to eye as much.'

'There are times when change is the best thing for us. As for tonight, you've rehearsed with us for three weeks now. You know the routines. You know the songs. All you have to do is relax. You're not going on alone and the girls will help you. The crowd will love Gyna Cologist, both here and at the Buckingham later.'

'You bet they will. She's a natural,' encouraged Mick.

'Thanks, Peter. For everything. I've found that I function at my best when I'm in a group.'

'Fair enough. You'll do fine. Just be ready by eight.'

'I will be.'

At eight-ten, a green light flashed over the door.

'What's that?' asked a slightly concerned Mick.

'Nothing to worry about, Mick.' I replied. 'We've had that installed as a reminder that's it time to go backstage. Everyone drew a sharp breath. 'Sheesh. How many times have you performed?'

'Not in such a detailed show or environment,' said Rory.

'You girls could go out there blindfolded. Let's go,' I encouraged.

I led them downstairs and quietly along the passage leading backstage. The strings of lights running along the floor allowed us, and the waiters, to see where we were going. The curtain between the kitchen and the showroom was now drawn and we slipped quietly past it. Whilst it was tempting to sneak a peek, I resisted.

Aidan, amongst other things, was also our stage manager.

Making sure that we were correctly wired for sound, he pointed us to where we needed to be. Mick and Rory waited stage right; Dean and Perry waited stage left. I took my position centre rear stage. There we waited.

Under the hem of the curtain, the spotlight appeared and a figure walked into it. The level of enthusiasm in the applause caught my breath. I knew how many people were likely to be there, still I was startled by their enthusiasm.

I heard Alex begin to speak.

'Good evening ladies and gentlemen and thank you for coming tonight.' The applause was quieter this time. 'As I haven't seen any ambulances arrive out front, I'm presuming the meal was to everyone's taste.' I smiled as titters permeated the audience.

'It's been about six months since this idea was first floated and after much blood, sweat and quite a few tantrums, you have before you the fruits of our labours, well the opening of our wallets at least.' The audience laughed and I breathed a sigh of relief. Alex was quite good in front of an audience.

'Apart from the excellent food, we all know why you're here.' The wolf-whistles and loud applause began. 'Without further ado, and to officially open the Lincoln Showroom, in her latest musical creation from the thirties and forties, I present to you, the madam of all madams ... Prissy DuPonce ...'

The curtain lifted and the lights came up. The crowd cheered very enthusiastically. The opening strains of '*Boogie Woogie Bugle Boy*' echoed throughout the room, from the band, and I stepped forward.

'Hellooooo daaarlings,' I cooed. 'It's so good to see you all here tonight. Oh look, there's even people I know. I'll have to keep it clean now.'

'That's never stopped you before, sweetie,' called a man from the audience.

'Ohh!' I replied, feigning embarrassment. 'I've just seen the very person who's taken *all* the fun out of it now.' I mockingly hung my head. 'My mother.' Tyco swung the spot to the booth where Mum was sitting, along with Nate, Terese and her husband, David, and Vaughan and his wife, Coralie. Mum waved the spotlight away and shook a motherly finger at me. 'Block your ears, Mum, it might be better.'

The music faded in preparation of our first number, 'Before we start, there's only one small announcement. The Poncettes have grown. Tonight we welcome to our happy family, Gyna Cologist. Make her feel welcome. She's a good girl.' I looked over to the band and nodded. They began the popular reworking of the opening music and we were into it. I decided to make the shows in the Lincoln Room as one continuous musical production. The banter I'd normally do between songs, I kept for the beginnings and endings.

At the end of the first show, I'm sure the crowd gathered in the cabaret room below would've been wondering what they were missing. I was astounded at the standing ovation we received, even after we'd left the stage and were going upstairs, we could hear it.

As we excitedly rushed into the changing rooms, I flicked on the large screen TV to see how the opening of the cabaret room was going. I sat down and watched as Alex hurriedly walked on stage, obviously out of breath. *He must've stayed and watched our first show upstairs.*

'Oh dear,' he said, bending over and holding a hand up to the audience. He made it deliberate that he was regaining his breath. 'Sorry about that, but I've just rushed from the showroom upstairs. If the sound-proofing worked, then you won't have heard how enthusiastic the crowd was.' I laughed along with the new audience.

'We've successfully launched the first of our two new rooms. Now it's your turn,' said Alex, being a little more official. 'You're in for a treat tonight ladies and gntlemen.' I watched as Alex responded to someone from the audience. 'Yes I know James is no lady, nor a gentleman for that fact, but he's still welcome.' The crowd laughed. 'Enough of me. You haven't come here tonight to listen to me prattle on about how it's taken six months of sweat and heartbreak over having to open my wallet so many times to get to where we are. It is with great pleasure that I introduce to you, here to officially open the Nedelina Cabaret Room, Zachary ...'

Alex left the stage and Zachary bounded on. 'Thank you for that warm welcome, Alex. Folks, isn't this a great place to be in?' The crowd responded. 'For the one or two of you that don't know me, I am Zachary Thumm, and I can give you the name of a good therapist after the show. I'm gay. I'm Jewish. I have a big nose and I unashamedly steal opening lines for my act.' He moved about the stage as the audience laughed. 'A funny thing happened on the way to the cir ... hang on, it's not a circus ... then again ...' Zach stroked his chin and comically pondered the thought. 'Damn it, it is a circus. Boys dressed as girls, gay Jewish comedians, how much more of a circus could you get? He was off and running, as was the cabaret room.

I sat back, took another sip of champagne and prepared to change. In the background, I heard the quips from Zachary and enjoyed the songs he sang about growing up in one of Melvegas' better suburbs.

'He's quite good,' commented Shelby.

'That's why we got him,' I said. 'Alex and I first saw him a year or so ago and when we decided to do this, I wanted Zachary to open the cabaret room.'

'He's the perfect choice,' added Samantha.

'We need to finish getting ready, there's the green light,' I said urgently.

Fur flew. Shoes were tossed unceremoniously into corners. Make-up was hurriedly touched up. We made it backstage with only moments to spare. Aidan wasn't impressed; I smiled, kissed him on the cheek, and said to him, 'We're here.'

Alex announced us again and the curtain went up on a scene from any of the luxurious ballrooms found dotted across high-class hotels from the 1940's. For this show, we were dressed in elegant, sparkled ball gowns. As the music began, we caroused and crooned our way through another twenty-five minute production of song and dance. On a few occasions, in true cabaret style, I left the stage and flirted with many a guest, male and female.

24. Endings.

By early October, the Lincoln and Nedelina Rooms were running better than expected. The success of the new venture was evident. Suddenly the rooms were booked solidly until after New Year. Thankfully, Aidan had planned well and the cabaret room had acts booked right through to the following February.

It also meant I had to work on new routines and rehearse them so that the many returning patrons didn't keep seeing the same old shows. I had decided to go with a sixties theme for October and we'd performed the first set of shows.

I'd revamped the line-up at the Buckingham as well and was beginning to use other performers, so that I wasn't always relying on the Poncettes. I introduced a development program that allowed me to help train new acts. These new drag queens I introduced on the quieter nights in the Lincoln Show Room. Perhaps it was my high professional standards, I'm not sure. Every new act was received better than I thought. Perhaps the standard at other venues was below par and I was the norm. Anyway, it was an interesting time.

Amidst all of this, I took a call one night from Torben, Rory's boyfriend. Between sobs, I managed to get out of him that Rory had collapsed at home and had been rushed to the Northern Hospital. I reassured Torben as much as I could and made sure he let the front desk know that we were family.

I hung up the phone. 'Alex, Rory's in hospital. Forget the dishes. We need to get down there.' I went to the foot of the stairs. 'NATE. Grab a jacket and be down here yesterday.'

Within minutes, we piled into the car and were driving as fast as we legally could, to the Northern.

'What's the matter?' It was the first chance Nate had to query the hasty exit.

'Torben rang to say that Rory collapsed and had been taken to hospital.' Nate drew a very sharp breath. 'That's all we know so far.'

'Is he okay? What's wrong with him? Will he be in hospital for long? What did Torben say? ...'

'Slow down, Nate,' I calmed. 'All Torben said was that he'd collapsed, nothing more. I know how close you and Rory have become.'

Nate sank back down and when I looked around, I saw him wringing his hands repeatedly.

I reached over and placed my hand on his. 'He'll be fine. We'll see when we get there.'

'We're here,' announced Alex, who dropped us at the emergency department and went to find a parking spot.

I wrapped an arm around Nate and we walked to the emergency room. Nate broke free and ran to Torben when he spotted him.

Torben broke down in my arms when I hugged him. 'Where's Rory at the moment?'

'They've taken him to intensive care. They mentioned something about his heart,' Torben replied amongst the sobs.

I turned to Nate. 'I know you'll want to go and see Rory now, however being in intensive care, that won't be possible for a while ...' Nate began to protest. 'Nate, listen to me please.' He looked at me earnestly. 'I want you to wait here for Alex. When he arrives, ask him to call the troupe. Also ask him to call Rory's parents; they'll need to know he's here. Can you do this for me?

I'll get you in to see Rory as soon as we're allowed to.'

'Okay,' Nate replied, wiping the tears from his eyes.

Comforting Torben, we left the emergency room. We walked up to the desk and inquired after Rory. The nurse gave us instructions and we made our way to intensive care.

When we arrived, we went to the nurse's station. As we walked along the hall, I noticed a lounge.

'Nurse, what can you tell me about Mr Rory Winston?' I asked when I had her attention.

'You are?' she asked.

'Peter Long-Smith.'

'Are you family?'

'Not specifically,' I replied.

'It's okay, I'm Torben, Rory's partner. He has my permission to make any enquiry necessary.'

'Very well,' commented the nurse.

'What can you tell me?' I queried again.

'Let me have a look,' she replied, reaching for a file. 'Let's see. An unexplained collapse, resulting in shortness of breath. We're waiting for results of a CT scan and x-rays. We've taken blood for testing and those results are due within the hour. His heart rate and blood pressure were abnormal. We're waiting for a heart specialist to have a look at him. I'd say that any further tests we will try and do tonight, otherwise they'll be scheduled for as early as possible tomorrow, depending on what the specialist has to say.'

'Thank you. Any information is appreciated,' I acknowledged. 'How many people are allowed in the lounge down the hall?'

'At this time of night, we'd prefer it be kept to a minimum,' answered the nurse.

'Thanks. We'll see the others downstairs then.'

'How many are there?' asked the nurse.

'There should be five others tonight,' I replied. 'I'm sure we'll be able to keep quiet. It's a fairly scary thing that's happened to a close friend.'

'We'll reserve the right to evict you.' The nurse smiled.

'Thanks.' I stepped into the lounge and sent an SMS to Alex to come to the intensive care unit once the others had arrived. I passed on the information I got from the nurse to Torben. About thirty minutes later, Alex, Nate, Mick, Dean and Perry exited the lift. I guided them to the lounge and they greeted Torben accordingly. I sat everyone down and passed on the information.

There were coffee and tea facilities in the corner and Mick made us all a hot drink. We sat around and began to talk about events.

'I thought Rory looked tired a few weeks ago,' said Dean.

'He always gives more than required,' added Mick.

'Yes he does,' I agreed. 'I never thought he was that run down.'

'Neither did I,' said Torben.

'What happened tonight?' I asked.

'We'd just finished dinner and were clearing away the dishes,' replied Torben. 'I'd taken a handful of dishes to the kitchen when I heard a noise. I called out but got no reply. When I came back to the lounge, Rory was in a heap on the floor, breathing heavily. I called the ambulance immediately and waited. They came very quickly and he was taken to the hospital. I had time to grab keys, wallets and phones so I could travel with him. As soon as he was admitted, I called you as they ran the preliminary tests.'

It was a long night and by midnight, Alex and I had sent the rest of the boys home whilst Torben had gone back to Rory's room.

'We'll call you if there's any change,' I encouraged. 'There's not a lot any of us can do here right now.'

When I came back in, Nate was resting his head on Alex's shoulder. 'One of us should take Nate home.'

'I'm staying here with Torben,' insisted Nate, sitting

upright at the mention of his name.

'You need to sleep properly,' said Alex.

'I want to stay.'

'We know you do, but Rory's in good hands.'

Nate began to cry. We hugged him, sat, and waited. At about one a.m., Torben came into the lounge.

'How is he,' called Nate, rushing to Torben's side. Alex and I were close behind him.

'He's okay. He's resting,' explained Torben. 'The doctors have had a further look at him, prescribed some medication via drip and are waiting for the results of some of the tests. They'll check him again in the morning.'

'That's sounds like good news then,' I said.

'I guess so,' said Torben.

'Do you want to come home with us, Torben?' asked Alex.

'No thanks, Alex, I'd rather stay here for any news.'

'We understand.'

'I want to stay too,' insisted Nate.

'You should go home, Nate,' urged Torben. 'There's not a lot you can do here. I'll be okay on my own.'

'One of us will stay with you,' I said. 'Alex?'

'Yeah, I'll stay. You shouldn't be alone,' agreed Alex.

'I'll be fine, really, guys,' said Torben.

'I'll stay,' insisted Alex, giving Torben a fatherly hug.

'Thanks, Alex.'

'Let's go, Nate,' I said.

'I really want to stay,' he protested.

'I'd prefer you go home and get some good sleep, Nate,' encouraged Torben. 'Do it for me.'

'Okay.' Nate hung his head. Torben came and gave him a hug.

I led Nate to the car, once I'd found out where Alex had parked it, and we travelled home in silence.

'You feel like some ice-cream?' I suggested as we approached a 24-hour supermarket.

'Not really,' he replied.

'Well I do,' I said jovially. I pulled into the car park and we got out. Nate followed me inside, dragging his feet. 'Let's see now,' as I made my way to the freezers. 'Hmmm ... choc-chip ... ooh, honeycomb crunch. Always my fave.' Out of the corner of my eye, I caught Nate shaking his head and grinning. 'Gotcha. Right, let's look at some bickies.' I marched off in earnest to the aisle where the biscuits were shelved. I began to walk up and down. 'Aww, look, here's a pack with cute little teddy bears on it. Ooh, I know, how about strawberry delight and we can dip those small teddy bear bickies?' At one stage, I saw a smirk pass across Nate's face. 'Gotcha again. You smiled. You do want ice-cream.'

'Perhaps. I get to choose the flavour?'

'Deal. I get to choose the bickies we use.'

'Okay.' Nate smiled happily.

We turned around and went back to the ice-cream freezers.

'I know it's hard and that you'd rather be at the hospital, but there really isn't much you can do other than sit. There's only so much sitting and doing nothing, one can do.' Nate laughed. 'We'll go home, eat the ice-cream, not tell Alex, and try and get some sleep.'

'If Alex ever finds out we had ice-cream without him, he won't be happy.'

'He's a big boy, he'll get over it.'

'Hey, you can't have ice-cream anyway. What about your diabetes?'

'How often do we have stuff like this?'

'Not that often.'

'Exactly.'

'Here we go, mango and macadamia,' announced Nate, holding up the tub of ice cream.

'Nice choice. Now, back to the bickie aisle.'

'Why didn't you choose when we were there just now?'

'I wanted to see what ice cream you were choosing,' I

replied. I waved my finger at him. 'You can't just have any old bickie with your ice cream?' We trundled off to where we had an extremely perplexing decision to make. More correctly, I minced back to the bickie aisle, whilst Nate dragged his feet. 'What to have ... Hmmmm.'

I stood there with my hands on my tilted hips. Nate just shook his head and walked away. 'Don't you walk away, young man,' I said in the queeniest possible voice.' Nate groaned. I flounced up and down in front of the sweet bickies. 'Decisions, decisions.'

'I'll be an old man before you decide,' said Nate quietly as he strolled past me.

'Cheeky wretch,' I retorted. 'I hope your kids are as cheeky as you are. Right, it'll be these ones.' I grabbed a pack of jam-filled funny face sweet biscuits. With the ice cream melting in Nate's hands, bickies held firmly in mine, we walked to the checkout.

As we approached the checkout, I could see the boy behind the counter smiling wryly.

'Is that all, sir?' he asked politely.

'Yes thanks,' I replied, in my normal voice. He looked up sharply. I smiled. As we left the supermarket, I turned to Nate. 'You know he heard me talking to you?'

'Yeah,' replied Nate and turned and smiled at the boy behind the counter. He looked away quickly. We laughed as we walked to the car.

Once at home, we settled on the couch, spoon in one hand, bickie in the other, and tucked in to the ice cream.

'Well that didn't take long,' I said thirty minutes later when the last of the ice cream was scooped from the tub.

'We should've had one each,' suggested Nate.

'Oh yeah, and watch my glucose levels go through the roof.' We laughed. 'We should probably go to bed and try to get some sleep.'

'I doubt I will, but I'll try.'

We cleared away the tub and spoons and walked upstairs. I had just cleaned my teeth and was changing for bed when my mobile rang. Nate came rushing into the bedroom. 'Hi, Alex,' I said. Nate was hanging off the doorframe so I indicated for him to sit down. 'Are you sure? ... Has a doctor seen him? ... Okay. Well, we'll get dressed again and come right down ... see you soon. Have you contacted the others? What about his parents? ... Ah, good. Bye, hon.'

'What's the matter?' Nate asked. I could see the concern on his face.

'Rory woke and sat up for a while, but then started complaining of severe chest pains. He was immediately reconnected to machines ...'

'And?'

'Get dressed so we can go back to the hospital,' I said simply.

'What's the matter?' Nate took hold of my arm.

'They don't think he'll last the rest of the night.'

Nate drew a sharp breath and I saw tears well up in his eyes. I gave him a hug and he sobbed. 'Go and get dressed.' Nate dragged his feet to his room and changed. Ten minutes later, we were back on the road.

We pulled into the car park and made our way to Rory's room as quietly and speedily as we could. When we arrived, it was a hive of activity. Nurses were moving about quickly. We could see that Rory had been connected to quite a few machines. As we looked through the window, we could see him lying there, his eyes closed peacefully.

I directed Nate to the lounge. Alex was there with Torben. Mick, Aidan, Dean and Perry arrived a few minutes after us. Another couple comforted each other in the corner. Nate went over to Torben and Alex came and gave me a hug.

'Are they Rory's parents?' I asked Alex.

'Yeah.'

I walked over them. 'Mr and Mrs Winston, I'm Peter Long-

Smith.' I held out my hand.

'Hello, Mr Long-Smith,' said Mr Winston, returning my greeting.

'Please, call me Peter,' I said. 'Rory's been working for me for a couple of months now. He's quite good.'

'Thank you, Peter,' replied Mr Winston. 'It was hard when he told us, but he was always different. Now this, it doesn't seem fair.' Mrs Winston buried her face in her husband's shoulder and cried again.

Just then, a doctor came into the lounge. 'Rory's awake again, only family can go in.' Torben looked at the doctor. 'That includes you.' The doctor smiled.

Everyone followed the doctor and whilst we stood at the window, Rory's parents and Torben went into his room. Rory's parents hugged him tightly. I watched as he reached out a hand for Torben, who stood on the other side of the bed and held it. My arm instinctively reached out and enclosed Nate in a reassuring hug. I felt him place his arm around my waist and nestle into my chest.

I couldn't hear what was being said, but it must've been dramatic as his mother reacted with shock. She cried some more and comforted her son. Rory's father followed suit. Rory then turned to Torben and gave him a huge hug and a kiss.

I grabbed Alex's hand and leaned into him. 'I think Rory has just said goodbye to those he loves,' I whispered.

Alex turned to me and smiled. 'I wondered about that too.' The three of us hugged a little tighter.

It was a few minutes before I registered that Rory was waving at us to come into his room. His parents stepped back and the troupe stepped up to his bed. 'Guys, I want to say thank you for all you've done for me,' began Rory, barely above a whisper, his breath shallow and strained. Mick and Dean began to protest. Rory held up his hand. 'Whatever happens, I won't be coming back to the troupe.'

'Of course you will,' said Mick, tears streaming down his

cheeks.

'I won't be, Mick,' continued Rory, taking hold of Mick's hand. 'If I ever do get the chance to go back on stage, it'll be a very long time. They're almost certain I've had a heart attack, but they're waiting for more test results.'

'Then why are we here now?' asked Dean.

'I wanted to see you all,' explained Rory. 'Even though I slipped into a coma for only a short time, it could happen again. I wanted to see you all before anything happened. Peter, Alex, Nate, it's good to see you too.'

Mick, Aidan, Dean and Perry moved away from the bed. Alex, Nate and I stepped up beside him.

'Nate, don't cry,' encouraged Rory. 'I'm so thankful for having met you. Don't give Peter and Alex too much grief, they love you, even I can see that.'

'What am I going to do if you're not around?' said Nate, the tears flowing freely.

'I'll always be around, if you remember me,' said Rory.

'I'll try,' said Nate. He hugged Rory like a brother.

'Peter, I can't thank you enough for giving me this chance,' said Rory.

'It was an honour to have you working with us,' I answered.

'I wish there was a way to repay you.'

'You don't have to, Rory, knowing you is a joy and a pleasure.'

Rory indicated for me to come closer. When I did, he kissed me on the cheek and hugged me. He did the same with Alex.

A nurse came into the room and urged all but Rory's parents and Torben to leave. We returned to the lounge and sat, a little stunned. I think we all realized that Rory had just said goodbye to us and that we'd never see him again.

I'm not sure how long we sat in the lounge, but we'd all dozed off on the couches and the floor. For some reason I sat up suddenly. I had this sense of foreboding. As I sat there, a cold shiver ran down my back. I looked up and saw Torben appear at the door.

By the look on his face, I knew what had happened. I woke Alex and then the others. Walking over to Torben, I hugged him. He burst into tears and sobbed into my chest. The tears flowing freely down my cheeks as well. Nate collapsed into Alex's arms. Mick, Aidan, Dean and Perry looked shocked.

'How long ago?' I asked Torben.

'About ten minutes,' explained Torben between sobs. 'We were chatting when he started to have trouble breathing again. We called for the nurses who attended him, but as they did, his breathing became shallower. They called for a resuscitation cart and they had to stop, as he wasn't responding. Eventually we asked them to stop. His mum held one hand and I the other and slowly we watched as he slipped away. Just before the end, he opened his eyes, turned to his mum and smiled. Then he turned to me, smiled, told me he loved me, closed his eyes and, and ...'

Just as Torben finished telling me what happened, Rory's parents came to the lounge. I let Torben go and hugged them both.

'We'd like to thank you for being here tonight,' said Mrs Winston. 'I know how much Rory appreciated what you did for him.'

'Thank you, Mrs Winston,' I said.

* * * * *

The funeral was the following Friday and was hard on us all. We let Nate stay home from school all week. I know that Nate and Rory were close and his death seemed to affect him more than anyone. After the funeral, Alex, Nate and I packed the car and we went away for a few days.

I decided not to perform for the next two weeks. I asked Aidan to contact Peachy Keen, to see if she could help. When she heard about Rory, she was more than happy to ensure my stages were graced with talent. Peachy herself hosted the Showroom and the Buckingham for me and passed on the details of Rory to the audiences.

* * * * *

Several weeks after Rory's sudden death, I received a call from his father. 'Hello Mr Winston, how can I help you?'

'I thought you might like to know what caused Rory's sudden passing,' replied Mr Winston.

'I wasn't expecting to know specifically. I certainly haven't heard from Torben about it.'

'We only found out today. It seems Rory had an undiagnosed heart condition.'

'Oh,' I said.

'Rory's grandfather died of a heart attack, so we knew there was the potential for heart disease in the family, but no one else has shown anything.'

'Very unusual.'

'Yes. The doctors seem to think that with all the work he was doing, and I'm not saying he was pushed, we know he enjoyed performing, that this may have precipitated his heart to react and in effect shut down over the twelve hours or so between the collapse and his passing.'

'He was a very hard worker and always gave everything he had to performing and rehearsal. Now I feel bad. We all noted he looked tired, but never thought ...'

'Peter, we don't blame anyone. Even as a kid, Rory was always running around. The doctors aren't sure why all of a sudden it should happen. They think that he could've just as easily lived for another twenty or thirty years without anything happening.'

'I'm sure we could've done things better.'

'Perhaps. All we know is that Rory was happy. Unfortunately, we never saw him perform. He only told us few years ago he was gay and we found it hard to deal with. I think we'd only just come to terms with it and were ready to accept him for who he was. My wife and I had spent many hours with therapists and other parents with gay children and they really helped us.'

'I'm sure Rory would've been proud. Would you like me to send you some DVDs of his performances with the troupe?'

'We'd like that very much. Let me give you our address.'

'I'll send them off to you as soon as I can.'

'Thank you, Peter.'

'Anytime you're in town, let me know and a meal will be on me.'

'Thank you again. That would be nice. I must be going, more family are coming over tonight.'

'I understand. Have you rung Torben to let him know the results?'

'Yes, we've spoken to him. Good night Peter.'

'Good night, Mr Winston. Thank you.'

I walked back into the lounge.

'What did Mr Winston want?' asked Alex.

'He was calling to tell me the cause of Rory's death,' I replied.

'What was it?'

'A previously undiagnosed heart condition.'

Alex nodded and I snuggled into him on the couch.

25. How Much for that Lady in the Window?

By the beginning of November, we'd settled back into rehearsing and peforming after Rory's death. The first rehearsal was hard as I made adjustments to the routines. I intended to wait until the New Year to look for a replacement, however the boys convinced me to start looking immediately. Yes, I had the talent program happening, but a number of them weren't ready and those that were had begun to move out on their own. Therefore, I placed ads in papers and magazines and of course on the walls around the Buckingham and Bucky's.

We'd also launched a new website, where applicants could register their details and access an application form. I had twenty applications by the end of the first week, and fifty by the end of the second. A lot of the applicants were those I'd trained. The response was so great, that I decided to stop running the ad at the end of the second week and placed a notification on the website indicating the same.

After I'd finished some office work, I went for a walk. It was lunchtime and I needed food. I came back and passed the window to the café. I stopped when I noticed a couple sitting at a table by the window.

'It can't be,' I said to myself.

The woman must've seen my shadow and looked back at

me. I'm sure she was about to indicate for me to stop staring. Instead, she froze mid-movement and dropped her food. She hurriedly drew her partner's attention to me staring at the window.

'It is them,' I called out. I raced inside.

'Jenny, it is you,' I called, racing up to her and sweeping her off the chair as she rose.

'Peter,' she replied. 'Look dear, I told you it was Peter.'

I put Jenny back on the ground and turned to hug Dave.

Let me explain who Jenny and Dave are. I've known Jennifer longer than I've known Alex. Jenny and I were at school together and even though we went to different universities to study, we were never out of contact. Soon after starting uni, I met Alex and then about a year later, Jennifer introduced us to Dave, who she'd met through friends at her unit

The four of us became very close friends. When Dave and Jennifer announced their engagement and we announced our willingness to commit to each other, we all decided to have one big ceremony. It was a remarkable sight. A bride and two gay men planning such a ceremony, it had to be spectacular. Dave surprised us all with some excellent ideas. We were each other's witnesses and the whole day went off superbly. Over the years, no matter what we did or where we were, the four of us were never out of contact for long. When Dave and Jennifer's children came along, we were there to support and assist.

When they told us they were moving to New Zealand, the tears shed could've filled an ocean. Email became very important and we spoke on the phone every couple of weeks. It also gave us a great excuse to go and see New Zealand a few times.

'Dave, it's so good to see you again.'

'It's been too long, Peter. Too long,' he answered.

'Are you here for a holiday? You should've told us.'

'We've moved back. Just this week,' explained Jenny, as I drew a chair to the table and sat down, I turned to the counter. One of the waiters saw and nodded, acknowledging my desire for a coffee.

'So, when were you going to tell us you'd moved back? How rude. Letting me gawk at you through the window like that,' I said with a flourish of my hand and a playful slap to Jenny's hand. 'Why this cafe, too?'

Jenny laughed. 'As I said, we only arrived this week. The kids are at home with mum so we could get a little bit of 'us' time,' she responded. 'As to this cafe, it looked quaint.'

'It's a bit late in the year to relocate whilst the kids are still in school, isn't it?' I inquired. 'Quaint! How rude.'

'We're home schooling them for the last few weeks. How is calling this place quaint, being rude?'

'That'll work. Now, what's the goss?' My coffee arrived as I asked the question. 'Barry, has this couple paid for their meal yet?'

'I'll find out for you,' replied Barry.

'If they haven't, make sure they don't. It's on me.'

'Okay, Peter.' Barry returned to the counter.

'You didn't have to do that,' said Dave.

'It's been so long, of course I did. How long is your mum staying for, Jenny?'

'A couple of weeks, so we can settle at home and so that Dave can adjust at work.'

'Let's catch up for a drink tomorrow night? Do you have contact numbers?'

'Here you go,' replied Dave, handing me a card. 'Drinks tomorrow would be good. The kids'll be disappointed they missed you.'

'There's always Sunday. We have much to catch up on, things to tell you. I'm glad you're back in town,' I said

'So are we, Peter, so are we,' said Dave. He looked at his watch and rose from the table. 'I'd better get back to work. Great to see you again, Peter. I'm looking forward to tomorrow night too.'

'It'll be memorable.' I smiled. *Oh, it'll be memorable.* 'I should get back to work as well. Talk to you soon.'

I hugged Dave and Jenny and watched as they walked away.

Racing through the building and up to my office, I began calling out. 'Al? Where are you? Alex?'

'What's the matter?' he replied urgently. 'What's wrong?'

'Nothing's wrong. I have the best news.' I leaned up against a doorframe to catch my breath.

'And why were you running? Why are you panting?'

'Running up stairs is nothing like a treadmill.'

'You're just getting old,' he responded, smirking. 'Now, what's this news?'

'Dave and Jenny are back in town,' I blurted out.

'You're kidding?'

'No, I just saw them in the café? They're gone now.'

'Why didn't you call me,' he chided.

'I was too excited. Besides, I've invited them out for drinks tomorrow night.'

'Before or after the show?' he queried.

'I didn't say.'

'Old and stupid. Must be time to trade-up, methinks.' Alex stroked his goatee.

'Yeah, yeah. Whatever,' I replied, walking on past him to my office.

'So what time did you want to get together with them tomorrow night?'

I turned and grinned at Alex. 'Well, my dear, let's have drinks with them *during* the shows.'

'During the sh ...' Alex suddenly smiled. 'You didn't tell them about Prissy, did you?' I shook my head. 'You evil, evil, man.'

I laughed wickedly and rubbed my hands together. 'Bring them in just before the first show at the Buckingham. I'll get Jenny up on stage and stir the living daylights out of her. Then turn on Dave, if they haven't worked it out by then.'

'As I said, you evil, evil, man.'

'Why thank you. I'll take that. Here's Dave's card. Give them a call later and set up the time.'

'By the way, why is it we haven't told them about Prissy? We've told them everything else, I think.'

'I'm not sure really. Perhaps it was because I wanted to keep it quiet for as long as possible and then forgot about it. We've been rather busy this year. First the Buckingham, then Nate, then Bucky's, then Rory. I guess it slipped my mind.'

'Although we remembered to tell them about Nate.'

'We weren't trying to hide that one. Oh well, we can fill in the rest of the details after the shows.'

'They'll kill you when they find out.'

'Perhaps, but they'll survive.' I got up from my desk and gave Alex a hug. 'I'm so excited now. I can't wait for tomorrow night.'

'It will be fun.' Alex stiffened suddenly.

'What's the matter?'

'If I remember, it's Jenny's birthday this weekend, or near enough to it.' He extricated himself from my hug and went to his desk. I saw him scrolling through his computer. 'Yes, here it is. It's Monday.'

'Even better. The perfect excuse to get her on stage. A birthday surprise.' We laughed.

* * * * *

I came from our shows in the Lincoln Room, and was changing for the first show at the Buckingham. 'I think next year, I'm going to roster what I do each week,' I said, puffing in my chair.

'Why's that?' asked Mick.

'Four shows a night is doing my head in.' Everyone laughed. 'Alternatively, I'll host one and perform in the other, changing from week to week, or month to month.'

'Might work,' responded Mick.

'It'd bloody better work.' I heard my phone vibrate to its heart's content on the desk. Picking it up with the longer than normal fingernails I had on that night, I carefully opened the SMS. 'Ah good, they're here.'

'Who's here?' asked Perry.

'Very old and dear friends of Alex and mine. I ran into them in the café yesterday and invited them to drinks with Alex and me tonight,' I explained. 'However, they don't know about Madam ... yet.' I winked.

Perry shook his head as the others groaned.

'Time to go girls,' I announced.

We clattered down the stairs to the room behind the stage. I made my ten-minute preshow announcement and we waited. On cue, the music for my first song, 'Gypsies, Tramps and Thieves' (of which I've been called all three), echoed through the bar. I caroused my way to the stage, flirting with the crowd.

Stepping onto the stage, I danced through the song. Looking out over the crowd, I spotted Alex, and right beside him were Dave and Jenny. They seemed to be enjoying the show. The song finished and I calmed the noise down so I could speak.

'Good evening, daaarlings. How are we all tonight?' I got the usual cacophony of sound. 'In fine voice, as usual.' I rattled off the notices and gossip for that evening.

'Now, a little birdie told me we have a birthday in the house? Is that true?' No one responded for a moment. I looked at Alex, who was waiting to see if Dave would do anything and when he didn't, Alex gesticulated overtly above Jenny's head. When she realised, she attempted in vain to dissuade him.

'We do have a birthday. Come on up here, sweetie. Let's see you.' At first Jenny refused, soon those around prompted her and she made her way to the stage.

She reluctantly walked on stage. 'Good evening, sweetie,' I said, planting a noticeable purple kiss on her cheek. 'What's your name?'

'Jenny.'

'When's your birthday?'

'Monday actually.'

'Very noice. You're a pretty one too. Girls, anyone of you got room for one more in your beds tonight?'

A few of the girls wolf-whistled. Jenny held up her hand to show me her wedding ring. 'What a shame. She's married, girls.' They made the required sounds of disappointment. 'Any children?'

'Yes, I'm happily married and have four children.'

'Four? You have been busy. Is your husband that good?' Jenny went bright red. 'How old are they?'

'Thirteen, twelve, nine and five.'

'No. You're not old enough to have a thirteen year old, is she folks?' The crowd responded accordingly. 'Now, where's your hubby?'

Jenny looked over to where they were and pointed him out.

'The one with the goatee?' I queried.

Jenny laughed. 'No, that's a friend of ours. The one next to him.'

I made to look as if I'd never seen him before. I whistled into the mic. 'Honey, you're one lucky woman. I'm sure I can find a boy to go home with him tonight and let you have a nice quiet night.'

Jenny didn't know whether to laugh or cry. 'I'd rather have him in my bed, thanks.'

'Well, sweetie, you'd better make sure he's kept close to you, you might lose him,' I goaded. 'Hey, I'd even take him home.'

Alex choked on his beer. I tried not to laugh. Thankfully, Alex was laughing again. 'I'm sure we've got something for you to blow, and I don't mean your husband,' I said. As I waited for the cake to arrive, I saw Alex lean in and whisper in Dave's ear. I watched Dave's jaw drop. He pointed to Alex and then to me and started to laugh. I smiled at him and moved on. 'On three ladies, and in your best Buckingham voice, one ... two ... three ... happy birthday ...'

After the song, I began to usher Jenny from the stage. 'Go and see Vince, he'll fix you up with whatever you're drinking for the rest of the night. You and your husband.' She turned sharply and looked at me, not sure what to think. I could see the question running through her mind; *Why should she shout us all night? She doesn't know us from a bar of soap.*

I brought out the girls and we performed our next few numbers. When they'd finished I came back on stage to close off before the finale. I was prattling on about notices, gossip and news, when I spotted Alex leaning into Jenny and whispering to her.

'Excuse me, young man,' I called out in Alex's direction. At first, he ignored me. 'I said excuse me,' a little stronger. Alex stopped talking and looked up. 'Yes, you. How rude of you to be speaking when *I* am. What's your name?'

'Alex,' he calls.

'Alex? Alex? Why do I know that name,' I said, mockingly tapping my fingers on my chin. 'Oh yes, you own this place with that gorgeous hunk of a man, Peter.'

'Gorgeous, yes, hunk ... I'll get back to you on that one,' he called back, smiling.

'Indeed. I'll make sure I let the other boss know that,' I chided. 'Now. What's so important that you need to be speaking with that lovely lady when I'm talking?'

'I was telling her a very special secret.'

'It had better be good.'

'Oh it is.'

'At least wait until I start singing, then I won't be so bothered.'

He closed his mouth and stood squarely to face me. I signalled for the music to begin, 'This is it for the first show, my lovelies. We'll see you in a little while for some more.' As the music swelled and I started to sing, I watched Alex go back to his whispering to Jenny.

I turned away to address another part of the crowd nearby and when I turned back, it was all I could do to maintain control. The look on Jenny's face was priceless. Alex and Dave were laughing. Jenny's eyes were wide, her mouth in a very good position to catch flies. Her drink tipped sideways and splashed the bare shoulder of the man in front of her.

I moved on as I saw Alex rescue the drink and Dave rescue his wife. She realised where she was and began to wave a finger at me. I blew her a kiss from stage and gave her a small curtsey. She began to laugh and got right into the song.

* * * * *

When the show was over, Alex brought them backstage.

'You evil, evil, man,' cried Jenny when they walked into the back bar.

I looked at Alex. 'I did not tell her to say that!' he insisted.

'Hmmm.'

Jenny gave me a hug and I gave her a matching purple kiss. 'Why didn't you tell us you were doing drag now?'

'In the beginning I wanted to keep it fairly quiet and I guess over time, we forgot about who did or didn't know.'

'What about yesterday? You could've told us then?'

'Yes, I could have, but I didn't.'

'You planned this, didn't you?'

'Who me? I'm an angel, or don't you remember?'

'Remember yes, angel definitely not.'

'Do you like what you see?'

'You're fantastic, with or without giving Dave and me a hard time.'

'It was too good a chance to pass up. Don't you agree, Dave?'

'Leave me out of this, but yes I agree,' he answered.

'That's okay for you to say, you weren't dragged up on stage,' said Jenny.

'No I wasn't, you were. The girls who wanted to take you home were licking their lips too.' Dave laughed. Jenny hit him.

'Don't you go off at her. I was watching the boys near us licking their lips at you when Prissy offered you up,' added Alex.

Dave turned and glared at Alex. It was Jenny's turn to laugh.

'Enough of that you two. It was all in fun,' I interrupted. 'I hope you're enjoying yourselves tonight?'

'I know I am,' responded Dave.

'I am too,' added Jenny.

'We'll catch up more when I'm done with the second show,' I said. 'I had better go and get ready. See you all soon.'

Once I'd finished the second show, I changed quickly and Alex, Dave, Jenny and I spent the rest of the evening, and into the wee small hours, reminiscing.

26. My Fair Madam

One day, sitting in my office, I found myself with a mind-blank over planning a new routine. I turned around and spotted some of the old accounting books on the shelves. I flipped through the pages and soon discovered that the Buckingham used to have a bar at the annual Melvegas Gay and Lesbian Arts Festival.

'Vince?' I said as I entered the bar, seeing him checking some orders.

'Yeah, boss,' he replied.

'I see in the records that we used to have a set up at the annual carnival day of the Melvegas Gay and Lesbian Arts Festival.'

'I think so.'

'For some reason I knew it by another name.' I leant against the bar, staring into the bottles behind the bar. 'What was it?'

'I remember,' stated Vince. 'We haven't done it for so long and I haven't been myself since my boyfriend at the time left me for someone else that day.'

'What a bitch!' I patted Vince on the hand.

'I'm better off without him.'

'You're single at the moment though aren't you?'

'Sadly.'

'It'll happen.' I smiled. 'TA-DA! I remember too. You first.'

'I couldn't. Ladies before gentlemen.' Vince bowed.

'Well that means that no one's gonna say anything because I doubt there are either of those are here right now.'

We laughed.

'Together,' I suggested. Vince nodded. 'On three. One ... two ... three ...'

'Queens on the Greens,' we said simultaneously.

'Look out, 'cause this queen's gonna tear up those greens,' I said.

'Here, here.'

We applied early enough and had been given an excellent location, which allowed us to include a stage. The boys and I had planned a summer spectacular.

By the beginning of December, I was being encouraged by the others to finish the process to replace Rory. I was resisting until after *Queens on the Greens*, but they urged me to bring in a replacement, as it was difficult adjusting the routines for three when they had become used to four.

I sat down at my desk and looked over the collection of applications I'd received. There wasn't really anyone in the development group I felt up to the task, so I decided to go for an existing performer. That narrowed my field to twenty. After further review with Alex, I narrowed it down to five. Interviews were arranged and each applicant was able to see me quickly.

The stand out was Aaron Marshall, whose alter ego was Cissy Gurlzblowse. Cissy was performing with Freda Mingle and I was worried that I was potentially taking two performers away from her. In the end, after a reassuring phone call with Aaron, I was happy to offer him the role. He began with us immediately and fitted in quickly and well.

* * * * *

The day for *Queens on the Greens* dawned grey and drizzly.

'Bugger,' I complained as I opened the blinds.

'What's the matter?' asked Alex sleepily, yawning and rolling over away from the window.

'Look!' I stated, one hand on a hip and the other waving at the grey sky.

'Look at what?' Alex replied without moving.

'Well if you roll back and looked out the window you'd see.'

I heard sounds of muffled coarse language as he rolled over and propped himself up on one elbow. 'What am I looking at, Sweetie?'

'That,' I pointed again.

'There's nothing out there.'

'Exactly. No sun. Only grey bloody clouds and freakin' pissy drizzle. You know what this means don't you?'

'That I'm about to roll over and go back to sleep.'

'It means,' I said, pulling the sheet off him, 'that I have to change my hair for today.'

Alex, naked as he was, suddenly jumped off the bed, grabbed me and dragged me back on to it. Pinning me down, he began to tap repeatedly on my chest. 'Now hear this,' he said between each tap, 'you will get up. You will have a shower. You will eat breakfast. You will pack the car as planned. You will paint on a smile, and if not, I will, and you will perform like you've never performed before.'

I tried to wrestle him off my chest, all to no avail. I stopped.

'Are you calm yet?'

'Yeah,' I replied. Alex relaxed his grip and as he did, I sprung up and unceremoniously dumped him on the floor.

'That wasn't fair,' he cried.

'Bite me.'

Alex crawled onto the bed towards me.

'I'm having a shower.' I left the bedroom and stomped my way down the hall.

When I came back twenty minutes later, Alex wasn't there. I dressed and went downstairs

'There's bacon, scrambled eggs, fried tomato and black coffee for you. Enjoy. My turn for a shower.'

'You'll have to wait.'

'For what?'

'The shower. Nate's in there.'

'Bacon, scrambled eggs, fried tomato and black coffee for two then.'

I smiled. 'Thanks, Sweetie. I'm sorry about earlier. I was a little disappointed at seeing the cloud cover.'

'What did you expect? It's summer, it's Melvegas. Anything can happen. For all we know, it'll be 45 degrees by mid-afternoon.

'I hope not, I'll have to use different make-up then.'

'Why do I bother,' said Alex, rubbing his head.

* * * * *

The fairgrounds opened to the public at ten but our stand didn't have to open until midday. Not that we had to bother, we'd left that up to Vince and the crew to arrange.

We met the boys at the Buckingham to pack the van with the costumes and, after loading, headed for the site of the fair. We drove right up to the back of the large tent we'd set up and before long, everything was ready.

The first show was at one. We came out dressed in our 'southern belle' costumes. I was in pale blue; the others were in pale pink, yellow, green and lilac. We pranced, danced and sung to a good crowd. I was surprised at the turnout really. Whilst still cloudy, it wasn't as grey and blue sky could be seen to the west.

After the show, I went and mingled with the fawning masses. As we left the backstage area, I reminded the girls that we had to return by two to be ready for the next show. To begin with, I grabbed a drink from the bar. After air-kissing Vince, I made my way towards the exit of our enclosure to try to get a look at some of the stalls and displays.

I think I managed to see about two of them. I really should've stuck with my original idea of keeping Prissy strictly to the stage, but as there was thirty minutes between shows, it wasn't practical to spend time removing all the make-up, only to have to begin again.

So there I was. Two steps forward, three steps back. Pictures. Fans. Even autographs, which was something I hadn't expected. I quickly scrawled a very flouncey signature, liked the look of it and smiled. Thankfully, it went over like a charm.

I looked at my watch and saw that it was time to return. I hung my head, turned around and walked back to our tent. That took almost as long and I was getting a little miffed at being stopped so much.

Vince saw me approaching the bar and had another drink ready for me.

'It's hell out there,' I complained.

'I noticed.'

I looked at him.

'Well, you didn't get very far. I'm surprised you even left the enclosure.'

'I wish I hadn't now.'

'Ah, the price of fame,' reminded Vince.

'Shut up!' I retorted. 'I wasn't expecting all this,' I added waving my hand around.

Vince laughed. 'Of course you did,' he said. 'Why else did you do it? The endless hours of applying make-up? Squeezing into dresses, wigs and shoes? Not to mention the hours of rehearsals.'

'Did I not, just this moment, ask you to shut up?'

Vince chuckled. 'By the way, Freda's been spotted at the fair.'

'Freda, you say?'

Freda. Freda Mingle. She was another drag queen out and about. If you haven't gathered, two of her former colleagues were now with me. I know if that had happened to me, I would have been pissed off, and from what I'd heard and been told she'd turned into a bit of an old has been. The two people who'd come to me from Freda, Gyna Cologist and Cissy Girlzblowse, both said they were better off with me. I daresay she'd turned up to let me know how she was feeling.

'Yes, Freda, I say.'

'Everyone's a comedian.' I shook my head. 'Keep an eye on her.'

'Yes Sir ... I mean Ma'am.' Vince saluted. 'Now, get backstage or you'll disappoint all your adoring fans.'

I looked at my watch. 'Shit!' I lifted the hem of my dress and made haste for the change rooms.

I entered backstage, laughing. The other girls were just about finished and I quickly changed in the costume for the next number. Just on two-thirty, I sent a message to the sound desk at the back of the enclosure and I heard our intro music start. Vince did his usual voice over and the music changed. For this number, we'd decided on doing a 'marching girls' routine. I'm sure that if my long deceased aunt saw me at this moment, I'd have red ears for months. We had the short white pleated skirts, white knee-high boot covers and matching white gloves. Our jackets were cropped, tight fitting and sequined with gold chains joining the twin rows of gold buttons. The crowning glory was our hats. Deliberately larger than a standard marching girl hat, yet equally as outrageous, and almost half a metre tall with black plastic brims. We had different colours – red, royal blue, emerald green, canary yellow and purple. Sticking out of the top of the hats were large white feathers.

It was hard performing. Not because of the costumes, but because of the cheers and raucous laughter coming from the large crowd. I saw some people wiping tears from their faces. By the end of the first song, which was difficult to finish, we were laughing.

'Oh dear,' I said, wiping a tear from eye, amid the cheers

and wolf whistles. 'I'm so glad that's over. Do you know how hard it is to dance in this get up?' I added showing off the costume. 'Are you having a good time?' the crowd cheered even more. 'Well, I'm glad to hear it. There's more to come this hour and another show at four.'

I moved to one side of the stage, away from the bar. 'Well, well, well, what's a nice young thing like you doing in a place like this?' I'd spotted a handsome young man sitting at a table near the front. I presumed the other man at the table was his equally adorable boyfriend. The boy I was attracted to had milky-coffee coloured smooth skin, short dark hair, neatly kept and dreamy green eyes. He wore a skin-tight pale blue t-shirt and jeans. If I didn't know better, I'd sworn I'd seen him on the cover of the monthly gay mag just before Christmas.

'I like your shows,' he called to me.

'Honey, I'll show you more than my shows.' The crowd laughed, as did he.

I stood and turned back to the centre of the stage. As I walked across, I spotted Vince waving and pointing towards the rear of the enclosure. I gracefully turned to face the rear of the enclosure and saw Freda making her way towards the stage. *That's all I need.*

Readdressing the crowd, I went on with a spiel about politics, gossip, sports and anything else that could be twisted to suit. All the time, out of the corner of my eye, I saw Freda getting nearer the stage. I did my best to ignore her.

Then she was there, right at my feet. The stage wasn't that far off the ground, a couple of steps at most, however being as tall as I am and as short as she is, she still looked small. Then it started.

'You bitch. You fat, ugly whore,' began Freda. The crowd around began to boo. It was then I realised she'd been drinking and was teetering on the edge. 'You're only this popular 'cause you slept with anyone and everyone.'

I could feel the heat rising in me, I decided just as quickly to wait it out, so I simply stood there and stared directly down at her. This unsettled her more.

'See, you don't even refute it. You're a cow,' continued Freda. 'You seem to have a habit of stealing my best acts. It's two now.'

I continued to look her in the eye.

'I've not had any work since Christmas. The one place I have left is not doing too well either. What do you have to say to that? Because of you, I'm ruined. You hear that, RUINED!' she spat those last words at my feet.

'Are you done my dear?' I responded politely and unflustered.

'If you're inviting me to continue, I can,' replied Freda.

'Not particularly, I was simply asking if you'd finished.'

'Probably not, but I wish you were.'

'I'll take that as a yes,' I responded, maintaining my calm and aplomb. 'If you please, I'd like you to leave our enclosure.'

Freda looked slightly stunned. The crowd was silent, witnessing the exchange and hoping for more than I was giving them. One or two boo-ed Freda as she was escorted away from the stage by security. She only waved angrily at them.

I turned my back to that part of the stage and faced the crowd. 'I'm sorry about the interruption folks. On with the show.' I waved my hands with flourish, fervour and wide arcs. 'I'd like to remind everyone of the shows at Bucky's with both the Lincoln and Nedelina Rooms. Bookings are essential. The current program should be on the tables, but are also available from the bar ...' I waved my hand in that direction only to see Freda force her way past some revellers and begin to walk towards the stage. I hung my head and rolled my eyes. 'Okay, what have I said this time? You know how crotchety I get when I'm disliked.' I stood with my hands on my hips. I walked to the side of the stage, away from where Freda would be and engaged a couple at a table. 'I saw you booing just now. How rude.'

'Oh no, no, no. It wasn't at you,' came the urgent and

apologetic reply. 'It was for her,' he added pointing in Freda's direction.

I turned deliberately to the look at the other side of the stage. Freda raised her glass at me.

'You mean *her*?' I replied, also pointing in Freda's direction. The young man nodded. 'It's already getting tiresome,' I added wearily. I crossed the stage. 'My dear, I thought I told you to leave.'

'I started to, but realised I wasn't done,' replied Freda.

'I think you're well and truly done, my dear.' The crowd laughed as Freda stumbled.

'Don't you know when you're not welcome,' called one patron.

'Go home, you washed up old hag,' called another.

'Boys, please, manners. In my arena, such quips are my domain,' I said, addressing the crowd, waving a finger at them. 'Honey,' I said, facing Freda, 'I have a show to do. Take a seat and I will be with you shortly. Then we can see if we can sort out your problems, although that may take some time.' Waving back security I hoped to get some peace.

Freda stumbled into an empty chair at a table near the stage.

'Don't go away folks, we'll be with you shortly.' I retreated backstage to wait with the troupe.

We performed our next routine and all the while there was loud, rude and obnoxious heckling emanating from Freda. I was proud of the girls that day. They held it together and performed as the professionals they had become. Towards the end of the routine, Freda had become louder and more obnoxious. I turned and saw security escort Freda from the enclosure, this time for good.

After the routine, I stayed on stage, amidst the applause. 'Thank you, my dears. You're too kind. Stop it.' I tried to feign embarrassment. 'All right then, if you insist.' I waved for more applause and got it.

'Let me through,' came a cry from the rear. I looked up. 'I'm not done here yet.'

I saw Freda attempting to reenter our enclosure. Security barred her way and one of them looked at me. I waved for Freda to be allowed in. I tapped my ear and held up my hand, indicating I wanted a hand-held mic. Tyco waved and I saw him duck out of sight. 'Well boys, talk amongst yourselves, I'll be right back.'

As I left the stage, I heard the crowd become hostile towards Freda. I went directly up to Gyna. 'I gather you saw Freda in the audience during the last routine?'

'I did.'

'So did I,' added Cissy.

'How are you both feeling?'

'Nervous. Worried. Concerned,' replied Gyna.

'Pretty much the same,' agreed Cissy.

I stood between them and placed an arm around each of their shoulders. 'My gorgeous children, you have every right to feel that way. You also have the right to be triumphant. Glorious. Faaaabulous.' I raised my arms and flicked open my hands. The others agreed with me. 'Because of that, I'll see what Ms Mingle wants.'

'Thanks, Prissy. Thanks to all of you.'

'It's been tough joining you. For a week or so, I had abusive calls from Freda. Sometimes she'd be begging me to come back.'

'We're more than happy to have both of you perform with us,' I encouraged. 'What would you like me to do?'

'With whom? Freda?' asked Gyna.

'Yes, Freda, of course,' I replied.

Gyna looked at Cissy, who nodded. 'Do what you have to.' Gyna declared calmly, but positively.

'I'll let her embarrass herself, firstly I'm going to continue like she's not there.'

'She doesn't like being ignored,' informed Gyna.

'I don't like being interrupted,' I said curtly.

Shelby and Sam sniggered.

'That's enough you two.'

As soon as I appeared from behind the curtains, the now larger crowd cheered heartily. 'Thank you, my Daaarlings. I must apologize for the delay in proceedings but I needed to have a quick conference. You're in luck today sweeties,' I continued, moving about the stage, 'I have some great prizes to give away. The main prize is a monthly dinner voucher for two at either the Lincoln or Nedelina Rooms for twelve months. Now, before you get too greedy, that amounts to one dinner per month for twelve months.' The crowd cheered and wolf-whistled. 'You need to fill in an entry form and we will draw it at the end of the day.' Hands rose rapidly and the guys from behind the bar ran around handing out entry forms. 'Right now, I have several dinners for two. I'll give away ... three, for now. The first three people who ...' people rushed the stage '... keep ya jocks on boys, I haven't told you what you need to do.' They walked away dejected, but hesitantly, waiting for my next instruction. 'The first three people who bring a Buckingham coaster, signed by Vince, who is trying to run away from the bar as I speak, to me at the stage, will win one of the three dinner vouchers. You also need to put your name, suburb and contact number on the back of the coaster.'

Well, it was mayhem. Boys ran to the bar, either carrying a coaster from their table, or grabbing those that had been placed on the bar.

'Don't worry boys, after I've given away the three dinner vouchers, the following five coasters that get handed to me will receive $50 dollar drink cards for the Buckingham.'

Within a matter of minutes, I had a flood of boys at the front of the stage. One of the bar boys, Drew, had come over to assist. I took three coasters from those being waved at me. I looked at the coasters and confirmed Vince's signature. 'I have the three winners for the dinner vouchers. They are Chris of Bankton, Jorge of Leighton and Magenta from Drewville.

Congratulations! We'll be in contact with you soon to confirm your prize.' I looked upon the happy winners. I handed those coasters off to Drew. 'Now for the drink card winners.' I took five coasters from the many still being waved at me. 'I have the winners of the drink cards. Jeremy of Rosdown, Kathleen of Eastcote – oh my dear, drunk dykes, not a pretty look …' the crowd laughed. 'Patrick from Leawood, Anna from Brigford and Carl from Burlong. Congratulations to you all. We'll have more prizes later.' Those remaining returned to their seats. 'If you have a signed coaster still and your name and details are on the back, place it in the box for the main prize,' I encouraged. 'You might still win.'

'That'd be right,' came the partially slurred voice from my right.

I looked over to see Freda sitting on the edge of the stage, as the crowd cleared away and went back to their tables.

'Excuse me?' I queried.

'I said, that'd be right.'

'What would be correct?' I continued.

'The only way you get people into your shows is to bribe them with prizes,' mumbled Freda.

'Is that so?' I replied, turning back to the crowd. 'Now that I've handed out …'

'Don't turn away from me when I'm speaking,' insisted Freda.

'Oh, I'm sorry,' I responded, 'did you have something to say?'

The crowd tittered.

'I haven't begun yet, you slut!'

I don't think anyone had heard Freda speak that way before. In the short time between our exchanges, Freda had certainly managed to down something more to drink. How much or what, I didn't want to know. The crowd went silent in a heartbeat. I stood still and slowly turned to where Freda was slouching. I felt the eyes of the crowd transfer between Freda and myself. I could imagine their thoughts. *What is she going to say? What's got into Freda?*

I stared at Freda for several moments. I turned back to my audience. 'Excuse me, sweeties, it seems I have to deal with something here at the front.' I walked deliberately to where Freda was, indicating to Tyco to bring the mic down. 'What is your problem honey?'

'You stole my best acts,' she replied.

'Is that all? You do realise that people can choose who they want to perform with?'

'Is that all? IS THAT ALL?' The anger rose in her voice. 'You come into town like a two-bit whore. You don't care whose toes you damage with your stilettos. Reputations are ruined because of you. You're a whore. A no good, talentless, cheap thrill-seeking two-bit slut!'

I stepped back and made sure people saw me look Freda up and down. I made a step sideways and took the mic from Tyco.

'You make a huge song and dance about how good you are.'

'I'm here to entertain, daaarling. Of course I sing and dance.' I gestured at the crowd who laughed, as much with me as at Freda.

'Stop making fun of me, bitch!' she cried.

'You're doing that well enough on your own, honey.'

Freda stood and unceremoniously stumbled up the two steps to get on stage.

'Let me give you a hand dear,' I offered, reaching out to assist her.

'Don't touch me!' Freda snorted, swinging her arm away from me, causing her to stumble and collapse onto the stage. She stood up and adjusted her aged and tattered frock.

I rolled my eyes and shook my head. Some of the crowd began to boo. 'Sweeties, please be nice to my *old* friend.'

'Who are you calling old,' Freda retorted and wobbled, I

attempted to steady her by reaching for her elbow. The crowd sniggered.

'I don't need any help, thank you very much.'

The force with which Freda wrenched herself away from my assistance, although not all that great, was still enough for her to spin around and topple off the stage. The crowd laughed hysterically. I rushed to the edge of the stage to see Freda lying on the wet ground, her dress scrunched up to her waist and her hat askew. People close to her tried to assist her to her feet. I also stepped off the stage to help her stand.

She stood, looking furious. 'Leave me alone. I don't need your help.' She was adamant and refused the help offered to her. 'You haven't heard the last of me, you bitch.'

Through all of this, I remained calm. I heard shuffling behind me and when I turned, I could see the troupe standing there, watching what was going on. Gyna and Cissy were standing next to each other, Shelby and Sam beside them.

Enough was enough. I clearly remember thinking that as I stood there watching. I genuinely felt sad for Freda. As I still had my earpiece mic in place, I turned, waving the hand-held mic, which Shelby came and took it from me.

'Ladies and gentlemen, I sincerely, and genuinely, apologise for this interruption to our show,' I explained. The crowd, silent throughout the latest exchange, applauded. 'Please, save that for the show. As soon as we're finished here,' I continued, walking towards Freda, 'we'll give you the show you came to see.'

Freda was still adjusting her dress when I stood beside her. I put my arm around her and whilst she struggled, I maintained my hold. I walked with her to the back of the enclosure. The more we walked the less she struggled and I could feel all her energy drain away. When we arrived at the exit, she proudly held up her head, brushed away a tear and strode away, albeit shakily.

I stood there for a moment and watched her disappear

into the crowd. I turned to my audience, every eye trained on my position, several mouths agape. 'As I said, it's on with the show.' I walked back to the stage, climbed the stairs, nodded to Tyco, gathered the now panicking Poncettes and returned backstage.

The music swelled. The effects started. The girls entered and I soon followed. The crowd cheered so loudly when we came on stage that I could see people outside the compound turn to look at what the noise was about. Tyco saw people approach and so cranked up the volume. Soon there was an even bigger crowd outside the enclosure all looking in on the show.

27. And The Winner is ...

I continued to our table and sat down. 'Do you think anyone knows?' I said, leaning in and asking Alex quietly.

He ran his fingers through his short blonde hair and smiled. 'I'm sure they do.'

I placed the most recent award with the other five on our table. It was starting to get embarrassing.

Between Alex and I (including Prissy), we took out;

Venue Worker of the Year – Alex;

Show of the Year – Prissy's 1940's Show;

Drag Diva of the Year – Prissy DuPonce;

Bitch of the Year – Prissy DuPonce;

Best Venue – The Lincoln Room;

Event of the Year – Opening of Bucky's.

'Big smiles everyone.' I looked up to see several flashes go off in quick succession. 'Can I get a photo of you two?' one photographer said, indicating Alex and myself. We obliged.

Alex handed the photographer a business card. 'As soon as you can, get copies to me.' The photographer nodded.

I started to laugh. Then Alex joined me. It wasn't hysterical, but we couldn't stop. We weren't drunk, even though it looked like it. I think Nate was embarrassed at the start, but then mum joined in. I was happy she'd flown in from Adelane for this event. As they say, if it wasn't for mum, I wouldn't be here. Soon Nate was laughing.

Now that Dave and Jenny were back in Melvegas, we invited them to join us for the Crystal Rose Awards. They looked at us strangely then laughed with us. Finally, Chrissy and Billie joined in with the frivolity. On the table next to us, away from the delightful drag queen and her feather boa, the Poncettes sat with their partners. As part of the opening show for The Lincoln Room, they received awards as well. They were beaming and they too joined in with the laughter. It must've been fifteen minutes before we stopped.

Wiping the tears from my eyes, I leant into Alex. 'You know why this is so funny, don't you?'

'I reckon I have a good idea.'

'Prissy's been on the scene for what ... about eighteen months?'

'About that.'

'The Lincoln and Nedelina Rooms opened only last August and here we are clean sweeping the entertainment section of the 'Rosies' for last year,' added Peter.

'I know, it's hilarious.'

'Can you imagine what they'll say when they find out at the Buckingham?'

'I reckon we can do drinks on the house for an hour or so,' informed Alex. Everyone raised his or her glasses happily at that thought.

'I'll tell Vince now.' I grabbed my mobile phone and sent Vince the text message. Actually, I made it six, one for each award, but decided not to say anything about the drinks.

After the sixth, he called me. 'Hello, Vince.'

'Are you kidding me or what?'

'No, not at all. We'll be there soon. You'll see.'

'The crowd's been growing all night.'

'How many have turned up?'

'About the size of a Friday night crowd.'

'That can't be. Queens don't come out on a Tuesday night.'

'Normally, no, but word got out about the number of nominations you received. I think they'll all here to see how it went.'

'Well, I'll be.'

'There'll be a riot here you know,' said Vince. 'We've just put the notice up on the screens. I'm surprised you can't hear the noise from there.'

I laughed.

'I was going to put it in the text message, but I didn't, drinks are on the house for an hour, maybe longer, when we arrive. See you soon.'

'Will do, Peter.'

'If this is the last award for the night, I say we head back to the Buckingham and celebrate.'

'Best idea I've heard all night!'

Twenty minutes later, the compere of the awards ceremony announced its official close and we packed up our six Rosies and headed to the Buckingham. Having a seven a.m. license at the Buckingham may not have been the wisest of decisions.

It was almost unbelievable. Six Rosies in one year. It'd never been done before, I checked. Not to mention the array of news and magazine articles that flowed during the week after the event. The most surprising call, though, came from a producer from one of the evening current affairs programs for an interview with Prissy. I declined, but the story still made it as a small article in the Friday evening program. As I sat watching the article, my mind was imagining the comments flying from the various stages across town that week.

www.ingramcontent.com/pod-product-compliance
Lightning Source LLC
Chambersburg PA
CBHW070010120726
47909CB00003B/865

* 9 7 8 0 9 8 0 3 8 6 7 2 1 *